THE MAKING
OF AN HOMBRE

Mike Tilman, a shanghaied crew-member of the *Yankee Star*, jumps ship at San Francisco, having accidentally killed the bosun. Now he must flee home before the 'Frisco lawmen catch up with him. But he becomes embroiled in a raid on the stage he is riding as a shotgun guard. Then he lands in the middle of a bloody range-war and it begins to look as if he will never make it home — at least not alive. Can he and his friends beat all the odds and win through?

ELLIOT CONWAY

THE MAKING OF AN HOMBRE

Complete and Unabridged

LINFORD
Leicester

First published in Great Britain in 2002 by
Robert Hale Limited
London

First Linford Edition
published 2004
by arrangement with
Robert Hale Limited
London

British Library CIP Data

Conway, Elliot
    The making of an hombre.—Large print ed.—
Linford western library
    1. Western stories
    2. Large type books
    I. Title
    823.9'14 [F]

    ISBN 1–84395–128–2

Published by
F. A. Thorpe (Publishing)
Anstey, Leicestershire

Set by Words & Graphics Ltd.
Anstey, Leicestershire
Printed and bound in Great Britain by
T. J. International Ltd., Padstow, Cornwall

This book is printed on acid-free paper

For the budding writers of
St Hild's Church of England school

1

Mike Tilman shivered and pulled his pea jacket tighter about him. It was almost full light. In an hour or so the sun would be climbing fast above the desert horizon, then would come the heat, oppressive in its intensity; sucking out every drop of moisture from his body. And with only a half-filled canteen of brackish-tasting water he would be gasping his last before night fell again, if his wild-ass hope didn't work out.

Mike was squatting at the side of the well-beaten trail of the Butterfield Overland stage line. Some twenty miles west lay San Francisco, and by his rough calculation of the time, the morning east-bound stage should be leaving the 'Frisco depot just about now. Mike was banking on the stage making an unscheduled halt to pick up an extra passenger. He didn't know how far a ride twenty dollars would take him but that was all he could afford, he couldn't leave himself flat broke.

He knew he was taking a high-risk gamble the stage would stop for him; if it didn't he had the unenviable choices of staying out here in this hellhole of a land until he shrivelled up and died of thirst, or try and hoof it back to 'Frisco, hoping to escape the hangman's noose awaiting him there for murder. Though in Mike's eyes it was an accidental killing. To avoid that grim fate he had to stay well clear of 'Frisco. Then at some town or other along the trail maybe he could find work enabling him to raise the money to make it back to New York, his home. He had read in the New York papers how the West was a golden opportunity for young red-blooded Americans to make their fortunes. Mike cursed. A red-blooded fella couldn't get any further west than San Francisco, and the only opportunity he had coming his way was an early, unmarked grave.

Even if he had the luck to get back to New York he would have to keep a wary-eyed watch for the law. He didn't doubt the 'Frisco law authorities would have wired the New York cops to arrest him for murder if he showed up in the city. Mike was confident New York's finest would never find him on his own territory, but he would meet that worry when he came to it. He had enough real worries facing him right now.

Mike scowled fiercely as he recollected recent events, coming to the conclusion his wild Irish pride had damn all to do with the way things had turned out for him. It had been the natural, simple matter of getting even, something his tough upbringing in New York had taught him to do. There, in the hell of the tenement slums the law of the jungle prevailed. A man fought to even up a wrong done to him any way he could: fists, feet, teeth, boots, clubs or other weapons. And he, Mike thought, had settled up the bill Olaf Larson owed him to the full. The fat-gutted bosun would never again use his rope end on any unfortunate sailor.

The first time he had clapped eyes on Larson had been months back in in the Clipper, a bar-cum-whorehouse close by the loading wharves for the San Francisco and west-coast bound merchantmen. To earn himself a few bucks, Mike fetched and carried for Abe Jackson, the owner of the bar. The day he had become a sailor there had only been three men bellied up to the bar. He had cast them a casual glance as he stacked up crates of beer behind the bar for the busy night trade. They were big, beefy-built, hard-faced men, especially the pork-bellied one wearing a blue jacket with brass buttons and a stiff-peaked cap. They were as tough-looking as any Bronx bully-boy he had seen.

Mike guessed the trio weren't out on a drinking and whoring spree but on the prowl around the bars and bawdy houses looking for likely men to make up a ship's crew. Any likely 'sailor' would feel the unexpected pain of a blackjack laid hard across his head. Then discover, when he came to, he was aboard a ship running south under full sail, to round the Horn then northwards on the long haul to San Francisco or some other west-coast trading port.

Mike had no fears the men would use their persuaders on him thinking he was likely material for a deck-hand, not in daylight with Abe coming in and out of the place. What he didn't know was that Abe had been slipped ten dollars to make himself scarce for a few minutes. Long enough for a new crew member, albeit against his will, to be signed on the general cargo schooner the *Yankee Star*.

Mike didn't suspect big trouble was about to come his way until he felt hands grabbing his shoulders and yanking him cursing and struggling wildly, across the bar top. His fighting back and cursing was cut off short and painfully, by a sickening blow on the head that laid him out cold.

A savage kick in the ribs brought Mike, groaning loudly, back to life, lying on the yawing, rolling deck of a ship. Another painful belt in the ribs cleared his fuzzy-headedness completely.

Wild-eyed, he glared up at his tormentor and saw it was the lard-bellied man he had seen in the bar, grinning down at him as he lifted his foot to deliver another kick. As a result of the fight-back-at-all-costs regime in which he had been raised, Mike sprang to his feet, fists swinging to draw the big man's blood, only to get knocked down to the deck again by a fist as hard as a mallet. Mike lay there, half-stunned, blood trickling from the corner of his mouth.

The big man grinned evilly. 'Bein' that you don't know shipboard rules yet, I won't haul you up in chains before the captain to face a possible hangin' from the yard-arm for mutiny by attemptin' to strike a ship's bosun. But that's the last warnin' you're gonna get. You knuckle down and take what I give you. My name is Larson and from now on in till we tie up at 'Frisco, when I say do this or do that, you do it at the double, or, by hell, boy, you'll find out why they call me 'Rope's-end' Larson. Now, on your feet and help those men aft lashing down that cargo. We'll be hittin' the grey-beards soon as we round the Horn.'

Feeling as though every tooth he had was loose, Mike staggered up on to his feet. Before he made it across the deck to where two of the crew were roping tarp sheets over open-planked crates, the ship rolled and pitched as it dropped down into the trough of a huge wave it had just crested and Mike felt the contents of his stomach rushing up into his mouth then spouting out in a greenish yellow flood across the deck.

'This deck ain't some New York back alley you can spill your guts in!' Larson yelled. 'I've had men on their god-damned knees scrubbin' these planks fit enough to eat their chow off! Hackman! Get this weak-gutted bastard a mop and a bucket and see he cleans it up real good. Then keep him workin'; he's in your watch!' Before striding aft, Larson gave Mike a parting lash across his shoulders with the rope-end, a blow Mike didn't feel being too busy heaving what little there was left in his stomach into the green rollers.

On the long haul north from the Horn, Mike was subjected to regular rope lashing and kicks from Larson for failing to carry out his orders promptly. Only the thought of how he would make Larson rue the day he roughed up a Bronx bucko kept the black hatred in his heart in check. His time would come, he promised himself, at a time of his own choosing.

Payback time for the bosun came when the *Yankee Star* was almost ready to sail on the return voyage to New York. Mike stood in the deeper darkness of the aft companionway hatch, well back from the port rail and the hissing glare of the wharf lights and the watch crew carrying on board the last of the deck cargo. Mike grinned wolfishly in the darkness as he tapped the belaying pin against the palm of his left hand. Larson was about to get one hell of a headache he hoped would last all the way to New York.

With his few belongings wrapped in a bundle at his feet, once he raised a lump on Larson's bullet head he would be over the side, his seafaring days over. A big city like 'Frisco would be bound to have a strong Irish community and a fellow Irishman would have no trouble in finding a job to earn himself the cash to make it back home by the overland route. The ship was sailing within the next hour so by the time the captain had worked out that his missing crewman could be responsible for laying out his bosun it would be too late to do anything about it. The ship and its valuable cargo couldn't wait in port for the next tide.

Mike tensed up, gripping the belaying pin tighter as he heard the heavy tread of Larson coming up the ladder. On stepping on to the deck, the bosun turned to walk along to the working party and almost bumped into Mike. He stopped in mid stride. 'What the hell are you doin' there?' he growled.

Then some sixth sense alerted him to his danger and his right hand flashed to his belt as Mike swung down the belaying pin. The crack of the stout peg hitting bone brought a smile of satisfaction to Mike's face.

Mike heard Larson give out a gasping groan then fall heavily sideways against the hatch then slide down to the deck to lie there in a crumpled, unmoving heap. He glanced anxiously at the working party to see if they had heard or seen Larson being clubbed. He breathed a deep sigh of relief when he saw the cargo loading was still going on uninterrupted.

Mike knelt down and began searching through the bosun's pockets for any money he could be carrying. He didn't think of it as thieving but as justifiable compensation for all the hell and hard work Larson had made him suffer. He felt a warm sticky patch on the front of Larson's shirt, a stickiness that only puzzled him for a few seconds. He drew his hand back, sharply, as though it had been burnt.

'Christ!' he gasped softly. 'Blood!' How could the bastard be bleeding from the chest when he had only cracked him on the head, he thought wildly? And, more frightening for Mike, the bosun seemed dead.

As he stood up, his foot kicked something that slid across the deck and landed in the scuppers with a metallic clatter. And then it all became clear to him. Larson had been quick enough to pull out his knife to defend himself, but, as he had fallen, had stabbed himself with it. Mike cursed. It was a bad situation he had landed himself in.

Though it could have been worse, he reasoned, Larson might have had time to stick his shiv into his guts.

He came to a quick decision; it would mean a major change in his plans. Once he leapt over the ship's rail he was not only a ship's deserter but a murderer. The way Larson had had it in for him for the whole trip he could never convince the captain that Larson's death had been an accident. Especially when it was discovered that the bosun had also suffered a head wound. The law would have a rope round his neck in a matter of days.

Mike figured he had to get as far away from 'Frisco as fast as he could, winning vital, life-saving time while the cops searched the city for him. He didn't want to take a chance that no one in the Irish quarter would finger him as a wanted man. He bent low over Larson's body and finished searching his pockets, cold-smiling at the macabre thought that if it was fated he was going to swing for murder they might as well add thieving to the charge. They couldn't hang him any higher.

Mike found a small roll of bills in the inside pocket of Larson's jacket. By its thickness and not being able to see the denomination of the notes, he didn't think it was the crock of gold at the end of the rainbow, but it would have to do, time was running out for him fast. The working party looked as though they had just about finished the loading and they'd be coming this way to get to their quarters in the bows. After a quick look along the deck and the wharf, Mike picked up his belongings and climbed over the rail, landing lightly on the dock side and ran, cat-footed for the dock gates.

Well clear of the dock area, Mike, by making a few discreet enquiries, found out that if a man wanted to leave 'Frisco other than on his two feet, he could hire himself a horse, bum a lift off the driver of one of the many freight wagons trailng south to Mexico, or by the Butterfield stage line, which ran a regular stage service as far east as Missouri. Mike crossed off travelling by horse, he couldn't ride one, even if the roll he had taken off Larson was big enough for the hiring charge. Likewise with hitching a ride with the slow-moving freight haulers. The cops would rope him in before he had cleared the city bountry.

It would have to be by stage. It would be fast-moving, as the driver had a timetable to keep. Though that still presented Mike with a problem. He couldn't walk openly into the stage depot office and book a seat. The depot would be one of the first places the law would check to find out if he was still hiding in the city. He would have to walk so far along the stageline's trail and take the risk the driver would stop for him. That seemed as good a plan as any to save his neck, Mike thought. It was no use worrying about things that may or may not happen. Events from now on in had to be taken as they came. He set off walking, eastwards.

'Barlow, Jackson!' the desk sergeant of the East precinct called out to the two patrolmen coming out of the squadroom checking their gear before going out on duty. 'Check the Irish bars: you're lookin' for a young Irish kid, goes by the name of Tilman. Tough-lookin' customer accordin' to the wharf superintendent. He's jumped ship leavin' a stabbed-to-death bosun behind him. He's new to the city and he'll not be rollin' in money so he might show up at some Irish bar askin' for a handout.'

'What about the eastbound stage, Sarge,' Jackson said. 'The kid could have done a little thieving before he jumped ship. He mightn't be so broke as you think.'

The sergeant glanced up at the station clock before answering the patrolman. 'The stage will have left by now and the depot will be all locked up. But I'll wire the marshal at Sulpher

15

Springs the kid's description. If the kid's on the stage he can hold him in custody until we can get out there and bring him back to stand trial.'

2

The stage rattled and bounced on the sun-baked hard ruts of the trail as Jed Lucus let the six-horse team have their heads coming down the grade regardless of the painful discomfort of his passengers bouncing about inside. Jed cursed and lashed the butts of horses five and six with his reins, urging them to even greater efforts. He was thirty minutes behind schedule in making his first stop and minus a shotgun guard.

Just before pulling out of the 'Frisco depot, Caldwell, his guard and relief driver, collapsed as he was climbing up on to his seat, complaining of severe stomach pains. One of the east-bound passengers, a doctor, told the depot manager Caldwell could be suffering from a burst ulcer or appendicitis, and needed urgent medical attention.

Jed had sniffed derisively. In his

considered opinion Caldwell's belly ache was the outcome of all the rotgut whiskey he had put away last night in the Golden Garter saloon.

'You'll just have to forgo a guard, Lucus,' Benson, the stage boss had told him. 'I'll wire ahead for a replacement to be waiting for you at Sulpher Springs.'

'Sulpher Springs!' he had said. 'Why that's a six-hour journey, road agents seein' there ain't a guard on the stage could jump me. And don't forget there's allus wild-ass Injuns lookin' for easy scalps to lift.' Jed cursed long and profanely under his breath. Benson, a Yankee dude, fresh from the East coast, thought the long haul from 'Frisco to St Louis, Missouri, was like riding a buggy along some tree-lined Connecticut turnpike. With a growled, 'Don't blame me if the stage rolls in at Sulpher Springs with me arrow-shot to hell and half the passengers dead.' He had kicked off the brake and lashed at the lead horses with his bull whip. 'Get haulin', you sonsuvbitches, we've got a schedule to meet!'

Ahead of him, Jed saw the lone figure standing on the left of the trail and eased back on the reins, then with his right hand drew the shotgun closer to him. Though he thought it couldn't be a hold-up *hombre*, it didn't do to take any chances. Road agents were generally bushwhacking bastards and a driver didn't know they were close by until his guard fell off the stage, plugged well and truly dead. Then, maybe two, three, of the murderin' scum would come ass-kicking out of the brush or a stand of timber, pistols blazing. And a driver, if he didn't want to be lying alongside his guard in the dirt, would haul the stage to a halt pronto and let them do their thieving unhindered.

The long first stretch of the trail was the badlands, furnace windswept desert, with no brush thick enough to hide a jack-rabbit let alone two or three riders. And whoever it was waiting on the trail had no horse and

Jed, who had had brushes with road agents for more than twenty years, had never known one desperate enough to attempt to rob a stage on foot in the middle of a desert.

A written rule of the stage company stated that stages must not stop between way stations to pick up passengers, fearing they could be a ploy by outlaws to rob the stage. Though there was another, unwritten but older rule, the plainsman's rule, the rule of the Good Samaritan, that anyone needing help on the plains or desert hadn't to be passed by unattended to.

A man crazy enough to be out here in the desert, on foot, definitely needed help, Jed opined. He yanked on the handbrake then pulled hard on the reins, bringing the stage to a screeching, shuddering, dust-raising halt. By the time the dust had cleared sufficiently for him to have a good look at his unexpected passenger, Jed had the shotgun hammers drawn back, ready for blasting out certain death at this close range. Kind-heartedness didn't mean acting foolishly. Any threatening moves from the man and he would stay out here in the desert until Judgement Day. Coughing and spluttering, eyes stinging from the throat-burning dust, Mike glimpsed an elderly, grey-bearded man wearing a droopy-brimmed hat as wide as his shoulders, and some animal's hide as a coat. And a gun pointed right at him. He raised both hands. 'I ain't lookin' for trouble, mister,' he said. 'All I'm lookin' for is a lift outa this desert before I fry. I've money to pay for a seat.'

Jed gazed down at a kid he reckoned was no more than eighteen or nineteen years old. In spite of his flattened nose and missing a couple of front teeth, which proved to Jed the kid had already found out life wasn't a bed of roses, he hadn't the mean-eyed look of an owlhoot. He spat a stream of brown juice over the side of the coach and thought by the kid's nasal Yankee manner of speaking, he was a longways from home. Judging the kid had no evil intentions in his heart he eased back the shotgun hammers and laid the gun alongside him.

He shifted his chaw into the other side of his mouth then said, 'It ain't company policy to pick up passengers who ain't booked a seat, but I wouldn't leave a dog out here in the badlands. Climb up alongside me.' He grinned a gap-toothed smile. 'Then, accordin' to my reasoning, you ain't a passenger.'

Mike smiled his gratitude as he scrambled aboard.

Jed gave Mike a narrow-eyed assaying look. He noted the short blue coat and the small bundle of his belongings resting on his knees. 'I know it ain't any business of mine, unless you're hankerin' to rob my passengers,' he said, 'but you sure ain't haulin' much gear to keep you goin' to where you're headin' for. You must be right desperate to get to that place to risk crossin' this stretch of territory on foot and ill-provisioned. It ain't exactly a land flowin' with natural goodness.'

A slow smile of understanding crept over Jed's face. 'You've jumped ship, back there in 'Frisco, ain't you, boy? I shoulda known by the cut of your jacket. I reckon some bully boys, on the East coast, by the sound of you, decided you'd make a sailor. I don't hold with their rough ways of persuasion at all. A fella could be drinkin' in some bars or enjoyin' the pleasures of a girl in a cat house then the next thing he knows a bunch of roughnecks are layin' into him and he's been dragged aboard some West-bound schooner.'

Mike didn't try to deny he had jumped ship, his pride wouldn't allow him to lie to a man who was helping him. Though he did wonder if the old man would still be as sympathetic if he discovered he had picked up a man branded as a murderer.

'Yeah, you're right, mister,' he said. 'I jumped ship. Though by my reckonin' a blackjack laid across your head in a New York bar don't make you a signed-up member of a ship's crew. So the first chance I got, that was in 'Frisco, I quit bein' a sailor. I'm hopin' to make it back to New York, pick up jobs where I can on the way to feed me and pay for the trip. I know it's a long way, but I'd rather walk every god-damned step of the way than do the return trip round the Horn on a hell-ship.'

'This line runs as far as Missouri,' Jed said. He grinned. 'I don't suppose your poke can take you as far as that.' He favoured Mike with another searching look. 'You seem a younker who don't scare easily, so I'll sign you on as a temporary shotgun guard. That'll get you as far as Sulpher Springs for free: eighty miles outa 'Frisco, a relief guard oughta be waitin' there for me.' He smiled again. 'Well outa reach of any press gang roughnecks.' Jed let out a bubbling yell and cracked his whip above the team's heads and the stage jerked forward in a flying start bouncing Mike hard back against the frame of the coach.

'I ain't fired a shotgun, or any gun for that matter, before, mister,' Mike said, when he got his breath back.

'Why there ain't nothin' to it, boy,' replied Jed. 'If any *hombres* come ridin' in real close, pistols fisted, you just point that cannon at them, pull back the hammers then let them have both barrels. Though hold tight to the piece, 'cos it's gotta kick like one of my team.' Jed cast him a sidelong glance. 'You needn't look so worried, boy, there ain't been no road agents workin' this stretch of the trail for quite a spell.' Keeping a straight face, he added, 'Though we could be unlucky enough to run into a bunch of mean-minded Injuns.'

Mike swallowed hard. Rope's-end Larson was a mean, bullying son-of-a-bitch, he thought, but at least he hadn't tried to scalp him.

'I'm Jed Lucus,' he heard the old man say.

'Mike Tilman,' he replied, clinging to the driving bench by the seat of his pants, as the stage rolled and creaked like the *Yankee Star* running ahead of a full gale. He held the shotgun tighter to his chest, gaze swinging regularly, and nervously, on both sides of the trail. He hadn't accidentally killed a man just to get sixty-eighty miles nearer to New York.

'We'll soon be clear of the desert, Mike,' Jed said. 'See that line of trees comin' up ahead of us? There's a crick of sweet water runnin' behind them. I make a ten-minute halt there, allow the horses to cool down and water. There's also tall grass and brush, givin' plenty of cover for the passengers, the three females included, to ease their bladders.'

Mike had prayed for some sunshine when rounding the Horn and had worked his watch on, and watch off, soaked to the skin with no dry clothes to change into. Now, after two hours of being baked by a fireball of a sun, and almost choked by the dust kicked up by the horses, a rest from having his ass bruised on the hard wooden seat and a wash down in a creek couldn't come too soon.

His dust-caked face cracked in a grimace of a smile. 'Mr Lucas,' he said, 'it's a wonder I ain't eased myself already the way my innards have been bounced around.'

★ ★ ★

Frank Allen and Al Weeks came on to the creek from the north-east and saw the stationary stagecoach on the far bank of the creek. They grinned at each other. So far, as they had drifted across California from Nevada, their pickings had been slim. A lonely sodbuster beaten unconscious, terrifying his family into handing over what few valuables and whatever else they possessed which Frank and Al could use.

While the pair weren't the most wanted outlaws along the Nevada and California border territory, warrants were out on them for cattle-lifting, store-robbing and two counts of suspected murder; they were building up enough tin-badge hassle against them to figure it was time they quit thieving in Nevada and try for a big killing in the California gold fields. Not by sweating swinging a pick or wielding a shovel, but by back-shooting some gold prospector who had already done the sweating.

'I don't reckon we'll be lucky enough, Al, to find that the stage's carrying a payroll strong-box,' Frank said. 'But the passengers oughta be carryin' enough cash on them and fancy gewgaws, watches and rings and the like, to grubstake us for a few days. And we could m'be use a coupla of those horses. By what I saw of the trail ahead from the last ridge it leads across some God awful territory.'

'We'll throw down on them when they're all about to get back on the coach,' Al replied. 'Then we've got them in a nice manageable bunch. If the shotgun guard so much as breaks wind, shoot him. The rest will get the message then that we ain't fellas to be taken lightly and start handing over what we want, fast, and without any trouble.' Al pulled out his rifle and swung down from his mount. 'OK, Frank,' he said. 'Let's go over that crick and get us ready to throw those folk one helluva surprise.'

Jed had pulled back on the reins until the team slowed down to a walking pace. When all the horses were up to their fetlocks in the water he drew them to a halt, still allowing his passengers to step out on to dry ground on the edge of the creek. He turned on his seat and yelled into the coach, 'Ten minutes' halt, folks! Stretch your legs, or do whatever you've got to do!' Straightening up, grinning, he said, 'And you too, kid. Go and settle your innards, I'll see to the horses.'

Mike waited until all the passengers had stepped down from the stage before dropping to the ground himself. Three of them were females, an elderly woman and two girls about his own age which he took to be her daughters. The three, after a short, low-voiced discussion, with much turning of the heads at the three male passengers, headed towards a thick clump of brush to the left of the trail.

Only one of the three men drew Mike's attention. A tall man wearing a light-coloured, light-weight, ankle-length coat over a blue cloth suit with a fancy-frilled collared shirt. His whole outfit, Mike opined, could have been bought in a New York tailor's shop. Though what marred the snappy-dresser's appearance for Mike was the well-stained broad-brimmed hat he sported, and the heavy pistol sheathed on his right hip belted openly across the waist of his store-cut jacket.

His Jim Dandy look didn't extend to his face; it was a lean, hard-eyed face. Larson's face had been hard, but with the sneering meanness of a bully-boy. The hardness Mike was seeing was the quiet hardness of a man who had his own way of seeing things done and God help the man who tried to force him to do otherwise. Mike reckoned he could be one of the gunfighters the West was full of according to the blood-and-thunder dime novels he had read back in the Bronx. Maybe, he thought, as he followed the three men into the trees on the opposite side of the trail to where the women had gone, the old driver would tell him who the tall man was, if he didn't tell him to mind his own business.

'OK, folks! It's time we were rollin'!' Jed, up on his seat, reins in his hand, called out.

Mike fell in behind the tall man coming out of the timber, wiping his face and hair dry with the sleeves of his jacket after dipping his head in the creek. The other two men were already at the stage. The tall man shortened his stride, allowing him to catch up with him. 'Kid,' he heard him say softly, without glancing at him, 'there's trouble about to hit us: two men are closing in on the stage.'

31

A startled Mike made to jerk his head round to see from what direction the trouble the tall man spoke of was coming. A snarled, 'Act naturally, kid! We don't want to alert the two assholes we're on to them,' stayed his nervous reaction, abruptly.

'They're there all right,' the tall man continued, conversationally. 'They reckon they're sneaking in but they're making as much noise coming through that patch of brush over yonder a deaf Indian could hear them. One thing's for sure, they're not coming in to pass the time of day with us. If I knew exactly where they were I'd cut loose at them, but if I start up any wild shooting those females could be in the line of fire.'

Mike was a sound-eared white man but he could hear nothing but the rushing of the creek and the wind shaking the tree tops so he could only accept the tall man's word that two men were prowling around nearby. 'What do you intend doin', mister?' he asked worriedly. 'Are you goin' to warn

that the tall man had asked him, an Eastern kid, to back him up.

Wendell Bannister, the tall man, had chosen Mike because he had the look of a kid who had come through rough times and was less likely to panic when the crap began to fly. He wasn't the ideal backup *hombre* but the old driver, a sodbuster, and a drummer, didn't leave him much choice, and he had damn little time to make it. The thieving sons-of-bitches would be showing themselves soon.

Wendell had a rep as a wild-assed, well-paid, shootist. His fast and accurate gun left him still standing whatever the odds he had taken on. A name to live up to so he didn't want it known that the pistolero, Wendell Bannister, had been robbed of all his valuables by a couple of penny-ante road agents. And that's the way it would be related, because he didn't want to take the chance of putting down two men with guns already fisted before one of them could pull off a returning shot with three females slap-bang in the middle of the gunplay.

The only risk Wendell worked by when the killing time came, was to himself, and the man, or men, he had been paid to shoot dead. Wendell thin-smiled. In this set-up a young kid was sharing the risk, by drawing one of the road agents' fire on to him. If he got a decent break the kid's risk would be brief, the ladies wouldn't come to any harm and his rep wouldn't have taken a fall.

The drummer and the sodbuster stood at one side, allowing the women to step into the stage first. Wendell, futher back, gave Mike, up alongside the driver, a slight 'get-ready' nod. Al, opining their intended victims were in a nice compact bunch, gave Frank a 'let's-do-it' nod. Both of them stepped into the open, pistols held at full-cock, Al favouring two guns.

'Now, if no one acts foolishly,' Al said, 'no one need get hurt.' He grinned wolfishly. 'We'll take what we've come for and be on our way before you've cottoned on to the fact you've been robbed.'

'There ain't no lowdown, thievin' drifters gonna rob my passengers!' Jed yelled, and grabbed for the Dragoon pistol he had stuffed into the top of his pants.

Frank fired once and Jed fell back on to his seat clutching at his right shoulder, face twisted with pain. The two girls cried out in fear and clung to their mother.

'Shotgun man,' Frank said. 'You kick that shotgun standin' alongside you down on to the ground. Any tricks and I'll not be so kind to you as I was to the old man. I'll blow your head clean off.'

Wendell thought his chance had come early but he saw the two-gun man hadn't been distracted by his partner's shooting and still held his pistols steady on them all. Cursing under his breath, he held back.

Mike had no intention of even moving. He was gripping the cut-down shotgun between his knees and only by huddling forward on his seat with the collar of his coat turned up was he hiding the two or three inches of barrel sticking up alongside his chin from the road-agent. He kicked out with his left foot and the stagecoach's shotgun thudded on to the ground. His wild Irish temper had the blood pounding hard in his temples at the shooting of Jed, causing him to forget his fears. He was welcoming the tall man making his move, getting the same feeling of grim satisfaction as he waited to crack open Larson's head.

'You in that duster,' Al said, 'just unbuckle that gunbelt slow and easy and drop it at your feet. No tricks, or I might accidentally put a shell through that timepiece you've got strung on a fancy gold chain across your chest when I put a coupla shells into your hide. And that would be a cryin' shame bein' as I've taken a fancy to it.'

Wendell, nerves taut ready for the split-second, life-or-death move, loosened his gunbelt and dropped it to the ground. Al grinned; everything was going smoothly. 'We might as well begin with you, mister,' he said. 'By the way you're decked out you must be well heeled.' His face hardened. 'For starters, hand over that watch and chain.'

Al didn't notice the slight twitching of Wendell's lips in a ghost of a smile. All he saw was the dandy dresser doing what he had been told to do, reaching under his coat for the watch. He slipped one of his pistols back into its holster and put out his free hand in preparation for getting hold of the fine watch. His smile was back.

Wendell's hand flashed out from beneath his coat and the small, single-shot vest-pocket pistol it gripped barked and flamed. Its heavy ball sent Al staggering back several paces with a hole in the centre of his brow and the back of his head a shattered bloody mess, dead before he hit the ground, still showing his cock-a-hoop smile.

Wendell let go of the derringer and dropped to his knees grabbing for his Colt in a desperate attempt to take on the dead road-agent's *compadre*; the kid, not having been involved in a gunfight before, could let him down.

Mike saw the tall man's right hand seemingly spout flame and saw the hold-up man go down. The suddenness of the tall man's action almost caught him unawares. He leapt to his feet swinging the shotgun across his middle and, hardly taking aim, fired. Some of the wildly aimed pellets peppered an alarmed Frank high on his left side as he was twisting round to bring his pistol on to Wendell, painfully bloodying his cheek and neck, paralysing his gun arm. Wendell fanned off two rapid shots at Frank while he was still on his knees, knocking Frank face down on the ground, dying as quickly as his partner had.

Mike gazed down at the second man he'd had a hand in killing. 'Sweet Jesus!' he breathed. How many more would be added to the total before he made it home, he thought soberly. No more, he hoped fervently. Though that hope would depend on what type of men he met on the trail. Feeling uneasy on his legs, he sat down. Killing didn't rest easy with him, even if in both cases it had been in self-defence.

'Good work, kid,' Wendell said, as he walked across to the stage. 'It was touch and go whether I'd pull off a shell before he did if you hadn't winged the sonuvabitch.' Then sensing how Mike was feeling, he added, 'Don't shed any tears over him, boy. Him and his pard were no-good bushwhacking thieves; kill if it suited their purpose. Take it as the law, me and you, caught up with them and made them pay for their wrongdoings.'

Wendell raised his hat and smiled at the elderly woman. 'I'd be obliged, ma'am, if you could tend to the driver's wound. Ladies can rustle up a piece of cloth that would make do as a bandage better than we men can. We males will see that the road-agents are buried. It wouldn't be a pleasant sight for the young ladies to have two horses with dead men slung across their backs roped to the rear of the coach all the way to Sulpher Springs.'

3

The stage rolled into Sulpher Springs one hour late, the sodbuster, used to handling plough horses, doing the driving. Jed, wounded arm strapped to his chest, was cursing the whole trip on how he would be damned if an itsy-bitsy scratch would prevent him from driving his stage to Carville, the end of his shift. Even if it meant holding the reins with his teeth.

'You needn't quit the stage,' Jed told Mike, as the coach drew to a halt outside the depot. 'You saved the company a helluva lot of embarrassment back there at the hold-up. The depot manager will be glad to give a free seat as far as you want to go.'

Mike declined the offer. 'I think I'll hang around Sulpher Springs for a few days, Mr Lucas.' He grinned. 'It'll kinda let my joints settle back in. But thanks for pickin' me up. And take care of that arm.'

★   ★   ★

Mike watched the stage pull out of the depot to restart its journey eastwards. He saw no sign of the tall man who had left the stage with him at the depot. Mike now knew he was called Wendell Bannister, a man who hired out his gun to men who wanted disputes settled in their favour.

He would have to find a cheap rooming-house, then tomorrow he would get down to the serious business of finding a few days' work. By the time the next east-bound stage came through his aches should have eased up and he would have earned enough cash to buy a seat on the coach for the next leg of his journey. It would take him a long time to reach Missouri, but it was easier on the nerves than riding shotgun.

Wendell, staying the night in Sulpher Springs, was standing at the bar in the

El Caso saloon. Come morning he intended riding north to Mile Creek, Nevada, where he had been hired by one of the factions in a range war taking place there. Wendell wished the Butterfield Stage Company ran a spur route to Nevada, being that he only rode a horse when he couldn't travel by coach or train. He turned, as a man brushed against him as he stepped up to the bar, a big, burly man, wearing a lawman's badge.

Marshal Hardy had heard of Wendell, knew of his rep as a notorious pistolero, and wasn't happy at him showing up in his town. Men died violently wherever he put in an appearance. Hardy could hear the mayor asking him to hand in his badge for allowing a gunfight to take placc in town, endangering the lives of law-abiding citizens. 'You ain't reckonin' on startin' any trouble in Mile Creek, Mr Bannister, are you?' he grated.

Wendell grinned. 'I never start trouble, Marshal,' he said. 'I'm paid to

45

end it. But, no, I'm headin' for Nevada tomorrow.'

Marshal Hardy breathed a deep sigh of relief. 'I'm right pleased to hear that, Mr Bannister. I don't want any shootin' in my town. Bein' you came in on the east-bound, took part in the ruckus back along the trail apiece, I heard, was there a young kid called Tilman a passenger on the stage? I've just got back into town and found a wire on my desk askin' me to check if he was on the stage. This kid they're makin' enquiries about has a knocked-about face. He jumped his ship after knifin' one of the crew to death. The depot manager don't recollect any kid gettin' off the stage but he could have jumped off before it came into town.'

'There was no kid of that description a passenger on the stage, Marshal,' Wendell lied smoothly.

'I thought there wouldn't be,' the marshal replied. 'An Eastern kid would get lost out here. He'll be lyin' low someplace back there in 'Frisco.' He gimlet-eyed Wendell. 'I'll look forward to you ass-kickin' outa town tomorrow, Mr Bannister,' he said. He turned and walked out of the bar leaving Wendell with the thought that young Mr Tilman — he had heard the driver call him that — had to be riding out in the morning as well, if he didn't want to be dragged back to 'Frisco in leg irons.

Killer or not, he was beholden to the boy for backing his play in taking on the road-agents. It had been touch and go whether or not the partner of the owlhoot he had shot down would have put a hole in him if the boy hadn't winged him, slowed him down somewhat. Wendell had kept the dead men's horses and guns, one mount for himself and, knowing the boy was staying in Sulpher Springs, he would sell the other and what cash he made on the deal he would hand over to him as a grubstake.

Now, Wendell thought, young Mr Tilman would need the horse to enable him to get out of town. And a rifle and pistol if he was going to survive out here in the West. He downed his drink and set off to find the boy who had supposedly knifed a man to death before the marshal accidentally bumped into him.

Mike, a mixer, decided he would have a looksee at Sulpher Springs' night life. He gazed out of the window in his room and smiled, wryly. It didn't seem as rip-roaring as New York with its Irish bars going full blast. Liquored-up Paddies, stripped to the waist, knocking hell's bells out of each other in the street in what the sporting papers called the 'Noble art of fisticuffs'. Mike fingered his broken nose, smiling. Head-butting, eye-gouging, iron-tipped boots in ribs and ball-grabbing some-how didn't fit in with the rules of the noble art.

First, he thought, he would have a bath — he could see a bathhouse opposite — have a nice long soak to ease the bruises on his back and ass from being bounced every way there was on the stage seat. Old Jed, Mike reckoned, must have the hide of a elephant. Then he would have a decent meal, the first since he had been shanghaied.

As he stepped outside on to the boardwalk and before his eyes got accustomed to the darkness someone grabbed his arm and pushed him back into the rooming-house. For one fearful moment Mike thought he was being shanghaied again. Then he heard a man say, 'It's only me, Mr Tilman,' and he recognized Mr Bannister's voice. 'It isn't safe for you to be on the street. The town marshal's had a wire from 'Frisco telling him to arrest you for stabbing a sailor back there. Did you stab that fella, Mr Tilman?'

'No, I didn't, Mr Bannister!' replied Mike angrily. 'That bastard, Larson, stabbed himself. All I did was to give him a crack on the head with a belaying pin, and he deserved it!'

Wendell looked hard at Mike, then said, 'Let's go up to your room and you can tell me about this fella Larson who got careless enough to stab himself to death with his own knife.'

Wendell sat down on the only chair in the room while Mike stood, telling him how he had been shanghaied and the hell Larson had put him through on the *Yankee Star*. 'I was waitin' to down him, to kinda get even for all the lashin's with his rope end he had dished out on me. Then I was goin' to jump ship.' Mike scowled. 'Then the bullying sonuvabitch had to fall on his own knife when I K.O.'d him. But no one on the ship would believe that. I couldn't see the port authorities wastin' much time searchin' for a sailor who had jumped his ship. 'Frisco must be full of suchlike deserters. But a 'murderer', well the hunt to track me down would be on for real. And with no friends in 'Frisco to lie low with I thought it would be healthier for me to make myself scarce. Then, when I'd sorted myself out, try to make it back to New York. You know the rest, Mr Bannister. And that's the goddamned truth whether you believe it or not!' Mike glared defiantly at Wendell. 'Are you gonna turn me in then?'

Wendell gave Mike an assessing look. He was an expert in judging killing men; he had sent many to where they would never be able to kill again. All he could see in the boy's face was righteous anger, not the shiftiness and bluster of a man lying to save his skin.

'I believe you, Mr Tilman,' he said. 'Though as you say, many wouldn't. My advice would be for you to keep moving. I'm heading north to Nevada in the morning; you're welcome to come along with me. Once you're out of California the law can't touch you. And you'll need to know how to handle guns. You already know what type of bad-asses frequent these parts. You can practise along the trail.'

'Where the hell am I goin' to get a horse and those guns you're talkin' about, Mr Bannister?' Mike said. 'I ain't exactly rollin' in dough.'

'Both of those dead road-agents'

horses and their gear are in the livery barn,' Wendell said. 'A horse and a set of guns are yours, count it as sort of a gift from me for backing me up in that gunfight, or as a reward from the stage-line for foiling a raid on their coach.' Wendell grinned. 'I can see now why you didn't press for a reward.'

'Thanks for the offer, Mr Bannister,' replied Mike. 'But I'm travellin' east, not north.'

'There's an old saying, boy,' Wendell said, 'that the shortest way to some point isn't always the speediest. California stretches a long way east from Sulpher Springs and there's no telling but the 'Frisco law *hombres* could have sent wires giving your description to other Butterfield depots. If you ride north with me, by noon tomorrow you'll be in Nevada, clear of the state law. And there's no stage depots north of here.'

'I ain't rode a horse before, Mr Bannister,' Mike confessed. 'And I'm gettin' the feelin' it ain't goin' to be a joyful occasion. But it'll be a damn sight pleasanter than bein' dragged back to 'Frisco and strung up for that sonuvabitch Larson's accidental death.'

'Good,' said Wendell. 'Meet me at the livery barn; it's just back of the saloon, at first light.'

'I was just on my way to the bathhouse,' Mike said. 'Then I was going to get some good grub inside me. Will it be OK? The lawman won't be hangin' about over there, will he?'

'No,' replied Wendell. 'The marshal will be in some saloon, or in bed. You go ahead and have your soak. I'll bring you some suitable clothes for the trail.' He grinned. 'To kind of take the eastern dude shine off you, OK? Then we'll eat together. To any other diner you'll be my pard.'

As Mike walked across to the bathhouse he knew for certain this time tomorrow, whether or not they had made it to Nevada, he would have the worst sore ass west of the Bronx.

4

Mike's pessimistic forecast of how he would be feeling was right, long before nightfall. The sun was still blazing down and his ass and lower back ached as though he was still hauling sail ropes on the *Yankee Star* battling to round the Cape. And every painful mile was taking him further away from New York. He cursed himself for his foolishness in not taking Mr Lucas's offer of a seat on the stage and risk the chance of being picked up by the law. Po-faced he bore his agony, not wanting to show Mr Bannister he couldn't take it.

Wendell guessed by the way Mike was holding himself in the saddle it had become a painful chore for him to keep on riding. He was also aware that if he asked him if he wanted a rest the boy's pride would have made him want to stay up on his horse until he dropped out of his saddle. Instead he said, 'We'll make camp here, Mr Tilman, there'll be water among those rocks. And it'll be an ideal spot for me to show you how to handle that Colt before we cross the Nevada line.'

Later, Wendell favoured Mike with a congratulatory smile. 'You're a natural shot with a pistol, boy,' he said. 'You're hitting so close to that stone that if it was a man you'd hurt him real bad. You needn't hesitate to draw on a man if forced to do so.' He grinned. 'Which is a mite more advantageous to you than wielding a belaying pin.'

Mike, ears ringing from the booming crack of the .45 Peacemaker Colt and eyes stinging with powder fumes, grinned with pleasure as he reloaded the pistol and slipped it back into its holster, belted on his right hip. For a half an hour or so after they had finished their coffee he had been pulling out the Colt and firing at a small rock Wendell had set up on a large boulder thirty strides in front of him.

'Don't worry about how fast you can yank out the pistol, Mr Tilman,' Bannister had told him. 'Speed will come with practice. One well-aimed shot does more damage than three wild ones. All pistoleros aren't fastdraw men; it's their willingness to shoot down a man that makes their name. If you have to pull out your pistol don't wave it about in the air as a threat, use it. A shell in a fella's hide gets your point over quicker than a whole book of threatening words.'

'Yeah, I know what you mean, Mr Bannister,' replied Mike. 'Me and some of the boys used to go round our neighbourhood hefting lengths of two by four and we didn't use them as callin' cards.'

'OK,' Wendell said. 'Lesson's over. There's no need to use up any more of your shells. Let's break camp, Nevada's no more than an hour's ride away.' He grinned. 'Though you may not think so now, you'll soon get your saddle-ass.'

Mike rode along no longer feeling hunted, more confident he could survive out here in the West, a land as alien to him as his forced stint on the *Yankee Star* had been. Wendell saying, 'We've crossed over into Nevada, Mr Tilman,' broke off his thoughts. The time was coming up when he had to fend for himself.

'Mile Creek, a town of sorts, lies just over that ridge ahead,' Wendell continued. 'It's better we should not be seen together.' Wendell twisted ass in his saddle to look directly at Mike. 'There's a range war going on north of here; gunmen are being hired to fight it. Pistoleros are a peculiar breed of *hombres*. Some get the urge to become the fastest gun in the territory, go out of their way to have shoot-outs with other pistoleros to build up their rep. There could be suchlike characters in Mile Creek who take a fancy to prove themselves by taking me on. If they see you with me they'll think you're a hired gun. And before you know it you'll be partaking in a shoot-out on Main Street.'

Mike grinned. 'I'll have to be on my own sometime, Mr Bannister. I thank you for makin' it your business to teach a city kid how things are here in the West. I ain't feelin' scared of this big, big land any more.'

'No need for any thanks, Mr Tilman,' Wendell said. 'You stood alongside me at the hold-up so it was only right and proper I should help you out. Out here we call it being beholden to a man. One further piece of advice would be to stay in Mile Creek for a few weeks until the hunt for you in California has cooled down. And ask around for work. As soon as the folk hereabouts hear your Yankee talk they'll not tag you as a hired gun. When you're ready to ride eastwards again keep north of the Nevada line until you reach Arizona. Then you're well clear of any California lawmen.'

Wendell didn't tell Mike he could

have bigger trouble ahead of him, Apache and bad-ass white-eye trouble. In spite of what he had told Mike about his shooting, Wendell didn't rate his chances of making his way safely across the hostile plains. Though he liked him, the kid's well-being wasn't his problem. He hadn't to ride to Arizona to meet up with trouble, the range war here would give him all he could handle.

Mile Creek, Mike noted, was a bigger town than Sulpher Springs though just as dead dog looking. He had parted company with Mr Bannister on the far side of the creek the town had taken its name from. They had shaken hands, wished each other best of luck, then the tall man had swung his horse round to come into the town from the north. He had waited, ten, fifteen minutes before heeling his mount into a slow, but painful hip-jogging walk, to ford the creek and enter Mile Creek by the California trail, resisting the temptation to flop down in the cool water of the creek and ease the burning in his raw-skinned ass. He drew up at the first saloon. It seemed the likeliest place to seek work, being that he was used to saloon work. Wincing, he gingerly slipped down from his saddle, leaning against the horse's flanks until his legs could bear his weight without too much pain. Mike had his hand on the saloon door to swing it open when he heard a girl's shrill cry of, 'Leave him alone, you big brute!' He turned sharply and saw that the trouble was taking place at a flat-bed wagon parked in an alley at the side of a general store on the opposite side of the sun-baked dirt track that passed for a Western town's Main Street.

A big, hairy-faced man was dragging an old, swarthy-faced man who had been loading the wagon, off the driver's seat. A young girl, dressed in Levis and a shirt, long black hair swinging loose, was tugging at the big man's arm in a vain attempt to pull him away from the driver. 'You have no right to stop us from buying supplies!' the girl shouted.

'We sheepherders have a right to live in the territory!'

The big man, holding the struggling driver with one hand, turned and laughed in her face. 'Missy,' he said. 'Sheepherders and greasers ain't got no rights in cattlemen's country.' And with his free hand he flung her back against the side of the wagon with such force Mike heard her gasp of pain. Body bowed dejectedly, the girl leant there, sobbing, all the fight knocked out of her. The girl-beater had the driver flat on his face on the ground and was kicking him.

Something snapped inside Mike; he was witnessing another Larson at work, could feel the pain of the kicks the old man was getting. Eyes blood red in wild Irish rage, his aches and pains forgotten, he ran across to the wagon, wondering as he did so what sort of spineless assholes passed for men in this collection of hog pens and chicken coops that called itself a town. There were three of them standing outside the store, one of them, by his apron, the owner, doing damn all to stop a man kicking hell out of a man old enough to be his pa and knock about a young girl.

Wendell, coming out of the livery barn, saw Mike run across the street and, by his grim, scowling look, guessed he was going to have more than words with the big man. He cursed. He had been hoping to ride into Mile Creek, get the smith to check out his mount's shoes, then ride out again before any interested parties who may be in town knew he had been there. The kid's rash act stopped him leaving — unless he wanted to see him beaten to a bloody pulp, or lying in the dirt shot dead, ending forever the kid's chances of making it back to New York. He knew the unsavoury rep of Max Lovell, the man kicking the old Mexican. A man who would kill anything that walked on two legs or four, if the price suited him. And enjoy doing it. Though Wendell had to admit the boy had balls to go up against a killing man like Lovell to save an old Mex from a beating, but he had no chance of beating the bad-ass to the draw. Wendell eased his gun in its sheath and walked along the street to even up the odds in Mr Tilman's favour. Before he got close enough to play his begrudging part in the trouble, Mr Tilman had began to settle it in his own way.

The girl, still leaning against the side of the wagon, still half-dazed by Lovell's blow, managed to give Mike a pleading, 'help us' look. Mike favoured her with a reassuring smile then his face steeled over as he came alongside the big man. He tapped him on the shoulder. 'Hey, you big ugly bastard,' he said, 'Ain't you got the guts to try your rough stuff on someone younger, or have you only got the backbone to beat up old men and young girls?'

Lovell, about to kick his victim again, spun round, fists raised, beefy face mottled red with mad-eyed rage. His wild dirty-mouthing was cut off short as Mike hit him with right and left stabbing punches that sank wrist deep into Lovell's belt-overhanging gut of a belly.

Lovell's breath came out in one painful whooshing gasp as he folded in the middle, hands clutching his stomach, low enough for Mike to head-butt him, breaking his nose in a shower of blood. Howling like a kicked dog, Lovell straightened up, hands now at his face to stem the flow of blood. Then, following the hard, no-quarter rules of the street-fighter that an opponent wasn't beaten until he lay flat on the ground unconscious, Mike dealt Lovell a vicious kick in the groin.

The big man gave one high-pitched womanish scream of agony before collapsing in the middle like a burst feed bag and fell flat on his face at Mike's feet. Mike, face flushed with victory, knew it would be weeks before the bully became a threat to the girl and the old man. He cold-smiled. It would be days before his swollen balls allowed him to get out of bed.

Wendell gave a low whistle of surprise. He had never seen a barn-built man hit the ground so rapidly without being shot, or clubbed by a pistol. The boy knew every dirty trick there was to know about rough-house fighting. What he didn't know was that his charitable act had landed him into a range war, unless he hit the trail to Arizona, pronto.

The ranchers who had hired his gun ran stock well north of here and their grievances were with another cattleman. What he had just witnessed was the age-old dispute between sheepmen and cattlemen. But why the need for hired guns? If Lovell was here, so were Cassidy and Peckham, his back-shooting partners. A normal ranch crew would soon clear a bunch of sheepherders off what they thought was their land. The sheepman always lost out in any trouble with cattle-men. Wendell shrugged. He would soon know what the set-up was in the valley. And he wasn't Mr Tilman's keeper. With-out making his presence known to him, he walked back to his horse.

Mike reached down to help the old man stand up and was rewarded with a '*Muchas gracias, señor*,' in a pain-racked voice.

'And from me too,' he heard the girl say, as she put a steadying hand round the old man's shoulders. 'If you hadn't come to our aid when you did, that brute, Lovell, would have crippled Señor Valdez.'

The girl took in Mike's hard, broken-nosed face and the sheathed pistol on his right hip. She gave him a wary-eyed strained smile. 'Are you another hired gun for the Double X?' she said, 'for if you are you've helped out two people you've been paid to run off their land; we're sheepherders.'

'Me, a hired gun!' Mike laughed. 'I ain't had this pistol more than a day, ain't fired it at anything but a rock. And I sure ain't heard of the Double X, whatever that is. I've just rode in to this dump to try and find a few days' work to help pay for my trip back to a real city, New York, my home town.' He nodded to the unconscious Lovell. 'I've had the same experience as the old man here from a big sonuvabitch like him. Coming across and beating him up seemed the natural thing to do.'

This time the girl's open smile was all sweetness and Mike saw the full beauty of her sun-bronzed face. And, in spite of her wearing well-worn pants and checkered shirt, he noticed she had all the soft curves he expected a young girl to have.

'I'm Kath Millar,' the girl said. Mike only half heard her, being occupied with blood-stirring images of how the girl would look in a dress. 'As I said,' continued Kathy, 'we are sheepherders and came into town to pick up some supplies but Mr Dolan, the store owner, he's the man standing there wearing the apron, told us our money wasn't any good any longer in Mile Creek. Mr Slade, he's the boss of the Double X ranch, told him not to supply any goods to us sheepherders.' Kath's eyes flashed with anger. 'I took no notice of him, and me and Valdez began loading the wagon with the supplies we wanted. Then that bully, Lovell, came on the scene.'

'We must go, *señorita*,' Valdez said, 'before more of Señor Slade's men arrive. Help me on to the wagon, *señor*.'

'I'd like to get the rest of the supplies, Valdez,' Kath replied. 'We might not be able to come into Mile Creek again, but I want to get you home to see if you've got any broken bones.'

'Tell me what you ain't got, Miss Millar,' Mike heard himself say. 'I'll get them in no time at all.' Then he asked himself why the hell he was getting himself involved in what Mr Bannister called a range war when he should be looking out for number one, getting himself organized for his long trip East. He put it down to the effects of being smiled at by a pretty girl, a pleasurable event he hadn't experienced since being hauled aboard the *Yankee Star.*

'I've ticked off what we've got, Mr, er . . . ' Kathy said. 'It won't be any trouble for you, will it?'

'Mike Tilman, late of the Bronx, New York City, Miss Kath. And it ain't no trouble.' He grinned. 'There could be trouble for that fella with the apron on if he don't co-operate.'

Dolan, the store owner, licked dry nervous lips as he gazed at Lovell's crumpled-up body. He was in one hell of a hot stew. The big son-of-a-bitch had told him not to supply any more goods to the sheepherders and that he would be hanging around just in case any of the sheepmen cut up rough at being refused supplies. Dolan gave a derisive snort. A young kid had cut up rough and Lovell had been stomped on good and hard.

Slade, boss of the Double X ranch, was the man who gave Lovell his orders. Slade, the biggest rancher, and the meanest talking man in the territory, would send some of his wild boys into town and burn his store down about his ears if he didn't quit selling stores to the sheepherders. Dolan did some frantic thinking.

Rancher Slade and the trouble he could sick on him was ten miles away. The asshole, Lovell, was lying useless on the ground, his manhood impaired somewhat and his nose knocked out of twist, and the ugly-faced short-assed kid who had hammered Lovell into the ground was coming over to collect what supplies he had refused the girl and the Mex. Dolan suddenly felt a shrinking, tender feeling at his crotch. The ghost pain almost brought tears to his eyes. Big trouble was right here on his stoop. Maybe Slade wouldn't come down hard on him when he heard of Lovell's painful downfall.

'I'll get those stores you're short of, Miss Millar!' he called out. Forcing his lips into a grimace of a smile he looked the fireball kid straight in the eye. 'Right away, sir, right away.'

'You do just that, mister,' Mike said.

'That young lady doesn't want to be more upset than she is right now by seein' more blood bein' spilt.'

He glanced back along the alley, not feeling so cool and in control of the situation as he appeared to the store keeper. The fight hadn't attracted any curious citizens, or men who could be local lawmen, yet. Even the two men who had been standing alongside the store keeper had made themselves scarce. Just like it was in the Bronx, Mike thought, take a powder before the law shows up and starts asking nosy questions.

An apprehensive Mike waited the few minutes it took for the girl's full list of supplies to be loaded before saying, 'OK, Miss Kath, it's time you were movin'.'

'You had better come with us, Mike,' Kath said. 'You've got yourself mixed up in our trouble and there'll be other ranch hands in town and when they find out you helped a couple of sheepherders they'll hunt you down on the trail.' Kath's face somehow lost its

71

beauty. She lowered her gaze from Mike. 'And, and they'll lynch you! You'll be safe with us.'

Mike was losing his tough image by the minute. He cursed himself for falling for a pretty face. That's how he came by his broken nose, admiring some other tough's girlfriend.

One bunch of men were already seeking him to sling a rope round his neck. Now, because of a pretty face, he'd have another bunch of men with the inclination to string him up. He sure had landed in the West with one hell of a bang. But what Kath had suggested made sense.

Mr Bannister had advised him to travel east, along the Nevada border. Once he lost sight of Mile Creek he wouldn't know in which direction he was riding, he would be lost. What he had seen of the West so far was one vast stretch of waterless dust and rocks. He could wander round in circles until he died of thirst and hunger, or got taken by wild Indians. He had to accept he was a babe in arms out here and had to learn new skills, fast, if he wanted to stay alive.

If he stayed with the sheepherders they could probably tell him what the trail to Arizona was like, where the waterholes and settlements were. Give him an even chance to make it back home. And, besides there was another reason for him wanting to go with Kath: in spite of all the trouble he had been through, he still hadn't lost his weakness for a pretty face. He smiled at Kath. 'Give me a minute to get mounted up and you've got company.'

At a steady ground-eating pace the wagon rattled along a trail that led south out of Mile Creek. And Mike got an insight in to the difference between the girls he had known in the Bronx and their Western sisters. Kath was doing the driving, handling the reins of the pair of horses with all the ease and familiarity old Jed had driving the stage team.

He also noticed that Señor Valdez

73

had a double-barrelled shotgun resting across his knees, in a state of alertness that had him casting watchful glances along his back-trail for signs of pursuers. And this was the fastest he had ever ridden and if he hadn't been in the company of a girl he had taken a shine to he would have been howling and cursing with pain from his blistered ass.

'There's no need to keep looking over your shoulder, Mike,' Kath said. 'We'll be at the settlement soon, long before any Double X hands drag themselves away from the saloon bars and get mounted up to chase us.' She was having strong feelings towards Mike, not just because he had risked his life to come to her aid, which she knew, was enough reason for her to have warm feelings for him, but also because Mike came from New York. He was a boy from another world. She had never known a boy who had lived more than a mile from her before. Like all her girl friends Kath had fantasy dreams of working in a big city store, wearing dresses, using perfume and soaking in big white tubs in bathrooms which had doors that bolted. All she'd had so far out of life was sheep, sheep and more sheep. Even her boyfriends smelt like sheep.

Kath sweet-smiled. 'Now tell me how a big city dude gets himself out here in Nevada — a dude who isn't comfortable sitting up on a horse.'

Mike favoured her with a lopsided smile. 'Uncomfortable ain't the word I'd use to describe the way I'm feelin' right now, Miss Kath,' he said. Then to his surprise, as though he was confessing his sins to Father Kelly at his local church, he told her all that had happened since he had been knocked out in Abe Jackson's bar.

Kath listened in wide-eyed awe as she heard about Mike's enforced voyage in the *Yankee Star*, the accidental killing of Larson, then his helping a hired gun to foil a stage robbery. Though Mike may be an Eastern greenhorn she knew already he didn't lack courage. Now she had discovered he had balls, as the boys in the settlement would vulgarly put it. Señor Valdez was sharing the same thoughts. The Yankee gringo wasn't a boy but an *hombre*, a man.

'Have you let your folks know you're still alive, Mike?' Kath asked. 'They could think you're dead not hearing from you for so long.'

'I ain't been able to stay in one place since I jumped ship to send off a wire,' replied Mike. 'And there's only Pa back home, and him and me don't hit it off. If I do make it back to New York I want to do it sneakily in case the law is lookin' for me there. I want them to think I'm out West someplace, or dead.' He smiled down at Kath. 'New York is one helluva big city, my territory, plenty places for a fella to lie low in.'

Kath hoped Mike would stay in Nevada but she couldn't see a city-raised boy staying in this big dusty land surrounded by sheep. She had known

nothing else and she wanted to get out of it.

Mike wanted to know more about Kath and this so-called range war. It didn't seem like the wars he had read about in the history books at school — when he had showed up at school. It was just then he saw his first sheep, scores of them grazing in a deep hollow on the left of the trail, and the two men armed with rifles standing on the rocks above them, grim-faced and alert. And changed his mind. They sure did look warlike, he thought.

The two guards raised their rifles in greeting, giving him a curious-eyed stare as the wagon passed beneath them.

'The settlement's just over this rise, Mike,' Kath said and jerked at the reins that set the horses into a high-stepping trot. Mike groaned aloud and followed in the wagon's dust. He had only known Kath an hour or so but she had caused him more pain than all the girls he had ever walked out with.

5

Rancher Morton Slade stood on the front porch of the big house drawing contentedly on a fat cigar. The ranch house was built on a tree-sheltered ridge giving him clear sighting north along the broad valley, over miles of good grassland he already owned. The valley stretched north for seven, eight, miles beyond his horizon, still good cattle-raising land, land he was determined to have for the growing herds of the Double X, as soon as he had cleared off the three small ranchers who grazed their few hundred head of cattle on it.

Once they got the grim message that as long as they stayed on the land he craved their barns would unexpectedly catch fire, and their herds would spook at night and take off in a leg-breaking stampede, giving their crews the ball-aching, time-wasting chore of rounding

them up, plus the unexplained shooting dead of some cowhand working out of a lonely line cabin, they would be eager to sell their ranches to him, at his knockdown price.

To the south of the valley, were the stinking sheepherders. Slade almost spat out his fine Havana in disgust at the thought of sheep chewing away at good lush longhorn feed. Even if he didn't need their land he didn't want sheep in the same valley, or even the same county. Slade couldn't make up his mind what breed of men he hated most, sheepmen, or ragged-assed sod-busters who ploughed-under good grass.

He saw a rider raising the dust coming up to the house, pulling up his mount in a haunch-sliding stop at the fence gate. Slade recognized him as Cass, one of the three gunmen he had hired to arrange the unfortunate accidents happening on the north ranges. Cass, along with one of his partners, Lovell, had been in Mile Creek making it plain to the tradesmen of the town

that it wouldn't be in their best interests to do business with the sheepherders. Not so much as a glass of beer or a shot of whiskey had to be sold to them.

If that type of harassment didn't convince the sheepmen that they weren't welcome in the valley and to pull up stakes and move back into California, then they would get a taste of what the northern ranchers were having to live with.

Slade's eyes narrowed in concern. He could smell bad news coming. Surely, he wondered, the sheepmen weren't foolish enough to be fighting back, thinking they could hold on to what they believed was their land?

'Trouble in Mile Creek?' he asked, impatiently, as Cass walked up to him.

'Could be, Mr Slade,' replied Cass.

Slade gave him a sour-eyed look. 'I'm paying you boys plenty to stomp on any trouble,' he growled.

Cold-eyed, Cass said, 'Me and the boys will do what you've hired us to do, Mr Slade.' Though opining Lovell

wouldn't be able to earn his due for quite a spell. 'You're bound to meet opposition in a range war. Men generally fight to hold on to what they think belongs to them. It's the man who heaps the most grief on the fellas they've got the dispute with who comes up the winner.'

'Yeah, yeah, I know that!' Slade snapped. 'What was the trouble in Mile Creek?'

Cass then told him of the beating-up of Lovell by an unknown kid.

'A young kid?' Slade said, looking at Cass in disbelief. And here he was thinking he had hired three of the hardest men in the territory. 'Is this kid a hired gun for the sheepherders?'

Cass shook his head. 'The store owner said he just came out of nowhere and beat the hell out of Lovell. And by the description he gave me of the kid, I ain't seen or heard of him before. Though he did say the kid spoke like some Yankee dude so he could be someone just drifting through the territory. But he did ride out of town with the sheepherder's wagon.' Cass's face twisted in a vicious snarl. 'Me and Peckhorn are intendin' to pay a visit to the sheepherder's camp, for no extra bounty, Mr Slade; if the kid's still there he'll get several .44 shells in his hide before he gets the chance to use his fists and feet.'

Though satisfied with the action Cass was about to take, he still close-eyed the gunman. 'I ain't heard it all yet, have I?' he said.

'The other trouble,' Cass began, 'ain't really trouble yet, Mr Slade,' Cass said. 'But it could be, and big if it comes.'

Slade had the overwhelming urge to ask Cass what the hell he was yapping on about. Ask him was there trouble, or wasn't there trouble? But seeing the hard man was still upset about a kid knocking the crap out of a buddy, which kind of took the shine off their reps as hard-asses, he held his peace and drew on his cigar to calm his impatience and waited for Cass to tell him more about this could-be-trouble situation.

'As you know, Mr Slade, we've been keepin' a lookout for any known guns ridin' into Mile Creek,' Cass said. 'And according to the livery barn owner Wendell Bannister rode in yesterday. Only stayed long enough to have his horse's shoes seen to then headed north along the valley.'

'Bannister?' Slade said. He swore. Bannister in the valley could mean big trouble for him. He knew of his rep as a top-notch gun fighter and, for a hired gun, his peculiar trait of picking and choosing whose side he'd take. 'I thought he had been killed months ago in Arizona wipin' out a nest of cattle-lifters?'

'The barn owner described him real good,' Cass replied. 'He even saw the chopped-down scattergun Bannister favours. If it ain't Bannister, it's his ghost.'

'Then those two-bit ranchers at the

head of the valley must have raised enough bounty money among them to have hired Bannister.' He spat out his cigar angrily, no longer savouring the taste. 'You and your boys,' he grated, 'will have to make sure that here in Nevada, Bannister's death isn't just a rumour as it must have been in Arizona.'

Cass was doing some thinking. Killing Bannister would put him in line for being the number one pistolero in the territory, a rep he craved for. The job was becoming interesting as well as financially rewarding. Naturally he wouldn't go up against Wendell alone, he had no hankering to be added to the long list of men Bannister had shot down. The son-of-a-bitch would have to face him, Peckham and Lovell, if he could move around and fire a pistol. He grinned wolf-like at Slade.

'We'll see that Mr Bannister don't upset your plans in wantin' your cows grazing along the whole length of this valley, Mr Slade,' he said.

6

Even by the standards of the two Western towns he had passed through Mike thought the sheepherder's settlement could only be called a dump. The shacks, some still under construction, were scattered along both sides of a creek. Beyond them were the sheep, hundreds of them, covering the grass like a blanket of snow.

Kath saw Mike's down-the-nose look and flushed with angry embarrassment. 'I know the settlement isn't as grand as the houses you have in New York,' she snapped, 'but these are our homes and some have fine furniture inside. One day, if we are left alone by the cattlemen this settlement will grow into a real town.'

Mike opined that if this place ever grew into a town in his eyes it would still be nothing but a collection of knocked-together shacks. But he had to curb his Eastern arrogant cockiness or he knew he would never get any closer to Kath. And after all there were plenty of brick and stone dumps in the Bronx; he had lived in one suchlike place. At least out here the air was cleaner and sweeter.

'And we do have a school,' he heard Kath say. 'Six miles along the creek, near the Californian border is a Jesuit mission, and three times a week a wagonload of children go there to be taught their letters and numbers.'

'I'm sure it will grow into a fine town, Kath,' he said lamely.

An elderly man standing on the porch of a shack somewhat more sturdily built than its neighbours and prettied up by having pots of flowers along the edge of the porch, smiled at them as Kath drew up the wagon alongside him. 'You're late, Kath,' he said. 'You had us worried. Did you run into trouble in town?' Mike got the same curious, 'who-is-he' glance from the man he took to be Kath's father, as the guards had given him.

'We did, Pa,' Kath replied, as she stepped down from the wagon. 'But Mr Tilman' — she smiled at Mike — 'kindly came to our aid. One of Slade's hired thugs began to beat up Señor Valdez though it ended up by him getting a thrashing from Mr Tilman.'

'You better come inside, *señor*,' Mr Millar said, serious-faced. 'Let Ma check you out to see if you've got any broken bones.' He stepped down from the porch. 'Here, let me give you hand, *compadre*, to get down from the wagon.' Mr Millar got a closer look at the boy who had come to his daughter and Valdez's aid. He could understand the boy shooting one of Slade's hired gun's but he didn't seem to carry the weight to beat up one of them. Though looks didn't tell you all about a man.

He smiled at Mike. 'You step down as well, Mr Tilman,' he said. 'You're welcome to sit down at our table and join us in a meal, after you freshen yourself up. And I thank you for helping my daughter.'

Mike, the inside of his thighs burning as though on fire, grimaced as he eased out of his saddle. 'Mr Millar,' he said. 'No offence intended but, hungry as I am I've gotta turn down your kindly invite; I ain't in a fit state to sit down anywhere.'

Trying hard not to laugh, Kath said, 'Mr Tilman is from New York, Pa,' she said. 'And he hasn't been riding long. He's kind of tender in parts.'

'You go and get a hot tub ready for Mr Tilman, Kath,' Mr Millar said. Then he told Mike he had some liniment that would take the sting out of his chafed limbs. He grinned. 'It don't smell as nice as French scented water, Mr Tilman, but it does the trick. Least-ways, it works on sheep.'

'Mr Millar,' Mike said. 'I'll cover myself from head to toe, and sideways with the stuff if it will ease the stinging.'

* * *

An hour later, a refreshed Mike managed to lower himself into a chair at the Millars' dinner-table. Mr Millar had spoken the truth, the axle-grease-thick, green liniment did smell anything but sweet, but it had eased his pains. And sitting next to Kath, who didn't seem to mind the strong smell, made him forget what pain he was still suffering.

After the meal, while Kath and her mother were clearing the table and washing up the dishes, Mr Millar took Mike out on to the porch, lit up his pipe then told Mike about the serious situation the sheepherders found themselves in, in a range war not of their making, or wanting.

'So you can see how ambitious Mr Slade is, Mike,' he said. 'Killing and burning until he gets every goddamned blade of grass, every drop of water in the valley for his longhorns. It's a bad business for us sheepmen. If the ranchers and their crews at the head of the valley can't hold off Slade, what chance have a few of us to stand up to him?' Mr Millar, stone-faced, drew on his pipe several times before speaking again. 'Slade has hired bully boys, you tangled with one of them, Mike, and a crew of twenty, twenty-five hard-bitten men. They could sweep us out of this end of the valley anytime he wants,' he said, bitter-voiced.

'Why don't he then, Mr Millar?' Mike asked.

'Because he doesn't want to be seen shifting us off our land too openly,' the sheepherder replied. 'Those tactics could get the county a bad name up at the capital; the governor could send in the army to protect us. No, Mike, he'll harass us until most of us lose heart and quit the valley voluntarily. Stopping us buying supplies in Mile Creek is Slade's latest move to tighten up the screws he has on us.'

'What about the law?' Mike said. 'The sheriff, marshal, or whatever name the law goes under out here? Can't he put a stop to Slade's dirty tricks?'

'The law here is cattlemen's law, Mike,' Mr Millar said. 'We woolly men haven't got a say in it at all.'

'Can't you do some deal with the ranchers Slade is trying the same tricks with,' Mike persisted. 'Kinda take on Slade together?'

Mr Millar laughed. 'You're more likely to get a mountain cat to lie down purring alongside a lamb than get a cattleman to even pass the time of day with a sheepman, let alone fight the same fight together.'

'It's worth a try, Mr Millar,' Mike said soberly. 'I know if someone had me by the throat squeezin' the life out of me, I'd fight like hell to get hold of any help I could. The Devil himself, and I'm a Catholic.'

'Yeah, well, that m'be so,' replied Mr Millar. 'But we sheepherders will have to play it as it comes.' He smiled at Mike. 'Now that's enough of our troubles, Mike. Kath told me you're trying to get back to New York. It ain't none of my business to ask what an Eastern city gent is doing wandering about out here in the first place but my advice is to start moving East again. This is our trouble, we don't want you dragged in it. You'll meet all the trouble you can handle on your trip. You've got one helluva stretch of wild country to cross before you meet the rail-road. I know Kath will miss you, but life isn't always what we'd like it to be. You go, Mike, and thanks again for helping Kath, and the old man.' He smiled. 'You might not think so, but your ass will soon toughen up.'

'It's part my trouble now, Mr Millar,' Mike said. 'Layin' out that bully ties me in with you sheepherders. The buddies of that fella will come seekin' me out to even up the score. That's what I would do if one of my buddies got beaten up.' He gave a cocky grin. 'If my bein' here puts a strain on your supplies I'll ride into Mile Creek and try and persuade that storekeeper to sell me some.'

Mr Millar looked hard at Mike. The boy could have signed his own death warrant but he was doing it willingly. It would be churlish for him not to accept his decision. He reached out and shook Mike's hand. 'Mr Tilman,' he said, 'you won't have to sore-ass it to Mile Creek for rations. When Kath knows you're stayin' she'll make sure you won't go hungry. She'll give me and her ma short rations. Though that don't alter the fact I think you're crazy to stay in the valley.'

Mike thought he was crazy also, but no more crazy than thinking he could cross the whole of the United States territory full of wild Indians and outlaws who would make an easy meal of a lone, Eastern dude.

Mr Millar took Mike round his neighbours' shacks introducing him to the other families. They were followed by several Mexican children. Mike jerked his thumb at the children. 'What gives with the kids, Mr Millar?' he said. 'Ain't they seen a New Yorker before?'

The sheepherder spoke to them in Spanish, the children answering him back in the same language, pointing and smiling at Mike as they did so, Mike not understanding a word that was being said or why he had become the centre of attention for the kids. Mr Millar grinned as he finished listening to the children. 'They've told me they've come to look at El Hombre.'

'El Hombre? Who or what the hell is that?' asked a puzzled-eyed Mike.

'Señor Valdez has told them about the way you fought that fella in Mile Creek, Mike,' Mr Millar replied. 'You're their hero, El Hombre, the Man.'

Jesus, Mike thought soberly, a hero. All he had done was catch a beer-gutted, out-of-condition man off guard. He would never get the same chance again. On the walk back to Mr Millar's shack, leaving his admirers behind, Mike realized he would have to practise drawing his pistol. Mr Bannister had told him he was more than a fair shot. He would, he thought, have to be a damn fast shooter as well. When trouble came at him again it would be shooting trouble and when it started he wanted to live, or die, justifying the kids' estimation of him.

7

Wendell, bending low in his saddle, picked out the fresh tracks of two riders heading in the direction he had come from. His hunch had been proved right. Somewhere ahead of him were two of Slade's men intent on killing another C L ranch-hand line man.

The sons-of-bitches wouldn't know that nemesis was coming along their back-trail. Wendell was about to earn his due.

The plea for help had come from rancher Al Brown and wired to him to Becksberg, Arizona, where he had helped to wipe out a band of cattle-lifters, men who were willing to kill to get their thieving hands on some rancher's longhorns. He had moved by then, back to San Francisco to rest up and let two bullet wounds, the fight with the rustlers had left him with, heal up.

The Western territories were full of young bucks wanting to make a name for themselves as pistoleros. By killing a noted one, especially one whose gun hand was impaired by a wound, fame would come easy. Brown's message was passed along the line by word of mouth by men in the same business as Wendell, until it finally reached him.

At the meeting with Brown and the other two ranchers threatened by Slade, he was told of Slade's tactics to secure the whole valley for Double X cattle, the barn-burning, night stampedes and the killing of a line man. He had said that he'd no great plan to scotch Slade's greed for land and that they had to accept it could turn into a real kind of war, with killings on both sides if they wanted to hold on to their ranches.

'Slade has at least three hired guns,' he said. Then he grinned. 'I stand corrected, gentlemen, two, for the time being. A young Eastern kid who I met on the stage on the way here put one of them down with a coupla punches and a kick as slick as I have seen from any man. All I can do is to range over your land and shoot any man I see acting suspiciously. It might force Slade to draw his horns in somewhat when he starts losing some of his crew, figure you've got hired guns on your payroll and that he isn't going to call all the tunes. If you tell me where your boundaries are I'll start patrolling.'

He had ridden out to the line cabin where the ranch hand had been gunned down. He saw the clear tracks of the two bushwhackers' horses leading in a direct line south, back to the safety of the Double X home range. His face hardened into a thin-lipped smile. As if he could see the killers, he knew they would come back this way again to try and pull off another easy killing. They could be already on C L land, aiming their rifles at some poor unexpecting ranch hand's back.

He dug his heels into his horse's ribs and set off in a wide swing southwards. If his reasoning was right he would be behind the sons-of-bitches, having all the edge.

Wendell rode fast but warily, opining he was by now riding across Double X land and didn't want to end up being the hunted. When he reached the stand of cottonwoods he had seen as a dark smudge on the far horizon from the line cabin, he drew up his mount and began looking for the tracks again, and found them, and the new tracks he hoped he would spot. He drew out his Winchester, levered a shell into the chamber, and laid it across his saddle ready for instant use.

Wendell liked to think of himself as an unofficial regulator, a trouble-shooter. As a hired gun, hired out only to the men who were having trouble heaped on them, he had shot dead enough men to have filled a small Boot Hill and it hadn't caused him one sleepless night. They had been men, in everyone's opinion, except the stomping men themselves, long overdue for being dispatched to where they belonged: Hell. Something the official law, for one reason or the other, had failed to do.

Wendell had lost his pa and older brother when he had only been a kid in a burning out and killing raid, the big man in the territory not wanting sodbusters on free range land on which he wanted to raise his cattle. Wendell then spent his bitter youth practising his skills with the pistol and the rifle until he was fast and accurate enough to begin building a rep as a pistolero.

Again Wendell had to trail fast but carefully, so as not to raise any give-away trail dust which could warn his quarry they were being tracked, or draw any trouble on himself, such as Double X ranch hands. Closing on a range of small hills, Wendell caught the tangy smell of woodsmoke and eased up his horse. Then away to his left, he caught sight of a bunch of cattle grazing in a grassy draw.

He dismounted, nerves screwed up tight, rifle held ready. He had lost sight of the tracks he had been following on the hard ground but he knew the two riders must be dangerously close. Dug into one bank of the draw was a timber-fronted soddy with smoke billowing out of its tin chimney. Its occupant, he knew, was the target for the two killers.

Wendell led his horse down into a nearby brush-strewn hollow and saw the two tethered horses. Their riders, he opined, would be bellied down close to the cabin, their rifles trained on the door ready to gun down the C L ranch hand as he came out to check on the cows.

There was no time for him to do some dirt crawling of his own to seek them out. The man in the shack could step out at any moment. He would have to think of some way of flushing them out, fast. Something that would look natural and not a man-made thing. Wendell glanced across at the horses, then grinned. No man who spent most of his waking hours up on a horse would take kindly to walking ten, twelve miles across rough, unfriendly territory where they could be shot on sight. If they saw their horses take off, Wendell was banking on them getting to their feet and chasing after them, quitting what they had come to do, and making them a good target for a well-placed Winchester shell.

Wendell loosened the tethering ropes and slapped both horses hard on their rumps. They took off in a high-kicking scrambling gallop up the bank side, he following close behind them to fling himself down on the rim, rifle to his shoulder.

His scheme worked. A man holding a rifle stood up from behind a rock in front of him and yelled, 'Hey, Jake! The goddamned horses have broken loose.' He began to run to try and catch them.

Wendell waited for Jake to show himself before he started to deal out death. Jake showed himself, waist high in a clump of brush away to Wendell's left, a target clear enough for him to snap off a killing head shot, knocking Jake back out of sight again. Then he swung his rifle on to the other killer, who was no longer running.

On hearing the shot he had stopped and turned to see his partner drop out of sight, dead. Wendell saw the look of alarm and indecision on his face, whether to run for it or take on the unseen shooter. His inner debate lasted as long as it took for Wendell to aim and fire. The man spun round, arms outstretched, rifle flying away, as the Winchester shell caught him high in the chest. Then losing his balance, he keeled over and hit the ground with a dust-raising thud.

Wendell stayed low, well aware the ranch hand in the cabin would have his rifle ready, trigger-finger itching, ready to blaze away at anyone he saw moving outside. He raised himself high enough to yell, 'You there, in the cabin! It's OK to come on out! The shooting's all over. I'm Wendell Bannister, I'm working for your boss, Mr Brown.'

'You show yourself, Mr Bannister!' came the shouted reply. 'Let me see just how friendly you are!'

Wendell stood up, slowly, rifle held down by his side and walked towards the cabin. 'Those two fellas I just killed,' he called out, 'were the same two fellas who killed your buddy at the other line camp.'

The shack door creaked open and the line man stepped out, smiling nervously. 'I thank you, Mr Bannister,' he said. 'If I'd stepped through this doorway five minutes ago I would have known nothing until I was hammering at the Pearly Gates askin' St Peter to let in a poor old sinner.'

'Think nothing of it, *amigo*,' replied Wendell. 'It's only what your boss is paying me to do. Have you got a spade in the cabin?'

'Yeah, a couple of them as a matter of fact,' the line man said, puzzled. 'You ain't thinkin' of raisin' a sweat plantin' those two bushwhackers are you, Mr Bannister?'

'I'm not burying them for any charitable reason,' Wendell said. 'You know Slade's hellbent on war hereabouts and he'll expect to see some of his crew shot. What he'll not expect is two of his men disappearing. And those lying out there are going to disappear, several feet underground. Then you round up those horses and take them back to the ranch, mix them in with the remuda. That ought to get Slade wondering what the hell's going on, m'be throw him off balance, give us a chance to hit him.'

The ranch hand's grin was real and wide. 'You get those horses, Mr Bannister,' he said. 'I'll dig holes for those two with the greatest of pleasure. Those sonsuvbitches intended me endin' up in a hole.'

8

Mike woke early. Though sleeping on a pile of sacks on top of a bale of hay in a feed barn was a great deal more comfortable than trying to sleep on the heaving wooden deck of the *Yankee Star* he'd had a restless night.

He had fallen asleep thinking of the pleasant hour or so sitting alongside Kath on her front porch, recollecting the warm blood-stirring softness of her thigh through the thinness of the dress she had worn at dinner as she brushed against him asking him how life was in New York. There and then, he had thought, he wouldn't give a damn if he didn't take a step nearer to New York than where he was sitting right now. Yet still those amorous thoughts didn't give Mike a peaceful night.

He had a few, more serious thoughts, chewing away at his insides. His blowhard pride for example. Telling Mr Millar he wouldn't sit still on his ass if someone was trying to grab him by the throat choking the life out of him. He would, he had boasted, do something about it. And his pride had been notched up still further by a bunch of Mexican kids thinking of him as a hero. They would be expecting some action from him soon or his big-headed Yankee pride would take a fall. And what would Kath think of him sitting here doing nothing to help her people in the battle against Slade? He wanted to stay here with Kath, but he didn't want her to think he was a yellow-belly coward.

A disgruntled Mike rolled off his bed, got to his feet and stepped out into the open. It was light enough for him to see the old Mexican, Valdez, squatting at a fire outside his shack. A little down the stream from him was another fire, gleaming fiery red. The settlement's blacksmith was also an early riser. Mike's face slowly hardened; he had come to a decision.

He stepped back into the barn and speedily put on his boots and jacket then buckled on his pistol belt and walked outside again. He had things to do before he left the settlement, before the Millars were up and about and told him it was crazy and dangerous to do what he had in mind — which, Mike had to admit, was crazy, but craziness sometimes paid off.

'Good morning, Mr Valdez,' he said. 'I reckon I must have been touched by your Western sun because I intend ridin' out to see if I can carry this kinda war to the big man, Slade. I don't know how the hell I'm goin' to do it, Mr Valdez, but I've got to try. I ain't used to lyin' back and lettin' the other fella get in the first hit.' Mike grinned self-consciously. 'The only thing is I don't know where Slade's place is and if I go out on that plain, bein' a city boy, I could end up in China. I was wonderin' if you could help me out, such as knowin' a track, a trail, whatever, along which a greenhorn could travel and get himself close to Slade's ranch without gettin' his head blown off, or lost.'

Señor Valdez had no doubts that the Eastern *hombre* was loco to try and fight Slade and his tough crew on his own. Though no more loco than he and the rest of the sheepherders were, waiting here, doing nothing but praying until Slade's men came with guns and flaming brands to drive them off their land. All the young Easterner was doing was getting himself killed sooner.

'There is a way, Señor Tilman,' Valdez said. He struggled on to his feet, still stiff and sore from his beating by Lovell. 'I will get my mule and show you the trail.'

'There is no call for you to risk your neck, Mr Valdez,' Mike said. 'It's my crazy idea.'

The old Mexican's back straightened proudly. 'When I was as old as you, *señor*,' he said, 'I fought alongside Juárez against the French in my country, Mexico. I am not afraid of danger. It is only my old bones and bad eyesight that is stopping me from taking up my gun to fight for my land again. And I owe you a debt of honour for coming to my aid in Mile Creek.'

'No offence meant, Mr Valdez,' Mike said apologetically. 'I'd welcome your help. It'll get me to where I want to be faster and safer, that's for sure.' He grinned. 'Though it makes me think there's more than an Eastern dude got struck by the sun.' Face serious once more, he said, 'Now there is something else I was wonderin' if you could oblige me with before we ride out. And I'll need the blacksmith's help as well . . . '

★ ★ ★

The settlement was beginning to stir when Mike and Valdez rode out. As well as several strips of jerky, a hunk of bread, a canteen of water and grain for his horse, Mike was armed with Señor Valdez's old shotgun, the barrels and

stock shortened by an obliging blacksmith with the ribald comment that the
doctored gun wouldn't fire as far as a
man could piss. Mike had grinned, but
said nothing. He had seen the deadly
work Mr Bannister's chopped-down gun
was capable of. And he could handle a
shotgun, more than he could his pistol,
if he was forced to use it in anger.

He was kitted out, he opined, as good
as he could be to fight in a way he
had never fought before. And he
wouldn't be the last man to go up
against wild odds for the sake of a
pretty face, he told himself. Though he
hadn't embarked on his crazy one-man
war just to look big in Kath's eyes. His
rough treatment by Larson had raised a
burning hatred inside him against all
bullies, and he couldn't allow such-like
characters to threaten people he classed
as his friends. In Kath's case, more than
a friend, he hoped. Mike gave a
sour-faced grin — providing he was still
alive when what action he hadn't yet
worked out, was done.

9

Valdez led Mike along a trail that edged
its way close to the western flank of the
valley. Sometimes, when the old Mexican judged the ground too open,
cutting into narrow canyon where the
trail snaked around steep rock faces
before entering the valley again. In one
such cleft, Valdez called a halt and
pointed ahead to a pillar of rock that
divided the trail.

'Take the left fork, Señor Tilman,' he
said. 'It will lead you on to Double X
land. You will see a low ridge running
eastwards. Nine, ten miles along it, is
Slade's grand ranch house. Ride close
to it, the trees and brush will hide your
trail dust. When you reach the water,
ride with greater care for the cattle will
be there, and men guarding them. Men
who will have orders from that dog,
Slade, to shoot down any strangers they

see on his range.' The old man smiled. 'I will leave you here: an old man mounted on an old mule will only be an extra burden to you crossing Slade's land. God be with you, *amigo*.'

'And with you, friend,' Mike replied, sober-faced. And as an afterthought added, 'And tell Miss Millar not to worry, I'll be OK.'

'*Sí, señor*, I will do that,' Valdez said, as he pulled his mule around to start the journey back to the settlement, and thinking of the lie he would have to tell the young Señorita Millar: how the boy she looked on warmly would do just fine. The young *hombre* was a long ways from being OK. He was quite certain the young boy was riding to an early grave. Señor Valdez crossed himself and muttered a few prayers for the soul of a true *hombre*.

Mike came out into the open, looking at the endless emptiness of the plain. He felt as though he was gazing across a grassy ocean. Fighting back his inner panic that he was out of his depth, realizing just how crazy his plan was, he took control of his nerves. How the hell could he get lost, he told himself savagely. He had the long guiding line of the ridge to his left and behind him the range of hills. All he had to fret about was keeping himself from getting shot by Slade's men. To further dampen his spirits, his thighs were beginning to ache. He hadn't got his saddle ass yet. Mike kneed his horse into a gentle canter closer to the ridge to use it a screen as Señor Valdez had advised.

★   ★   ★

Billy Jayhawk cursed his ill-fortune, but as befitting the stoicism of his mother's blood race, the Paiute, he watched impassive-faced as one of his captors threw his rope over a tree branch above his head.

The other ranch hand grinned at Billy. 'Well, Billy,' he said, 'you've stole your last calf from Mr Slade's herd. You're about to pay a permanent visit to your Injun happy huntin' grounds. That's if those red heathen allow 'breeds there.'

Billy glared back at him, lips curled in what he believed was a Paiute warrior's kiss-my-butt defiant snarl. He wasn't a wild part-Indian; he didn't go on burning-out-sodbusters raids, scalping and raping white-eyes. All Billy wanted to do was to live as his mother's people had before the coming of the white-eyes.

He had the urge to roam free, take a calf from the Double X when he was hungry, as he would have killed a buffalo if the white-eyes hadn't killed them all off in the territory. What was one miserable maverick to a man who couldn't count the number of longhorns he possessed? The white-eyes owed him the calves, the sons-of-bitches hadn't paid the Paiutes for the land they ran their cattle on. Slade thought otherwise, taking his cattle was a hanging matter.

Mike caught the glimpse of water

through the trees and heard the snorting of cattle. Remembering old Valdez' warning about men being close by the cattle, he dismounted and pulled the shotgun from out of his bedroll to scout ahead on foot. He saw three horses and three men standing under a lone tree beyond what he took to be the same creek that ran through the sheepherders' land. Closer to the creek was a big bunch of cattle.

Mike thought there was a good chance of swinging by the men if he moved further along the creek, using the cattle as a shield as he crossed it. He was about to go back to his horse, when, taking a final, longer look at the men at the tree, he saw one of them was swinging above the ground, legs kicking wildly.

'Jesus wept!' Mike gasped and face twisted in shocked anger, he ran, high stepping through the shallow water of the creek, all thoughts of his great plan of sneaking on to Slade's land and raising a minor hell for the rancher forgotten.

The ranch hands, enjoying seeing Billy Jayhawk, eyes bulging, twitching and jerking like some landed catfish, didn't see Mike high-tailing in on them until they heard the blast of a shotgun, then lead hail whizzing ominously above their heads, showering them with leaves and snapped-off twigs. Hands let go of the lynching rope as though they had been burnt, and clawed for pistols. Billy dropped to the ground gasping for life-giving air.

'Don't pull out those pistols!' Mike snarled. 'You murdering sonsuvbitches! There's another load pointed straight at you!' He stood there, straddle-legged, covering them with the shotgun that Mike was pleased to see he held steady-handed. He had the satisfaction of seeing both men turn towards him with their hands raised high.

Both men exchanged significant get-ready glances as they weighed up their chances of throwing down on the kid holding the shotgun on them, a kid who hadn't the balls to cut them down with his first shot. As hard men they knew that it wasn't every man who could pull off a killing shot, even to defend himself. They played for time, waiting for the kid to relax his guard.

'Me and my buddies ain't what you called us, kid,' one of the men said, smiling at Mike as though he was close kin. 'That 'breed lyin' there is a cattle-thief and we're entitled to string him up.' His hand inched down to his pistol.

'What you bastards are entitled to do and what you're gonna do ain't the same thing,' Mike said. 'What you're gonna do is to shed your pistols and rifles and get up on your horses and ride back to your boss. Tell Slade he ain't about to get things all his own way.'

The ranch hand laughed. 'Who the hell are you, kid?' he said. 'Do you think one cut-down scattergun is goin' to scare Double X crew? Why, we'll come huntin' for you and stomp you into the ground with no sweat at all.'

His hand was almost at his pistol butt. He gave his partner another sidelong glance, trying to keep his 'got-you, boy', grin from showing.

Billy Jayhawk, neck rubbed raw by the noose, but breathing easier, saw the ranch hand's ploy. Nerves jangling at his closeness to death and the likelihood he could be soon dancing on air again, he screeched hoarse-voiced, 'Shoot the bastard! He's goin' for his gun!'

Mike's reactions to the shouted warning, his own nerves stretched tight, was to jerk wildly on the shotgun trigger. Held loosely the shotgun bucked in his hands, firing wild. The ranch hand, who had been confident of getting the drop on the kid, howled with pain as a spray of shotgun pellets tore into his legs, blood rapidly darkening his pants.

'You sonuvabitch!' he sobbed, hardly able to stand. 'You've crippled me!'

Face set hard, Mike thumbed reloads into the shotgun chambers and, snapping the barrel shut, covered the other ranch hand. He cursed under his breath. He had landed headfirst into the range war, not the way he had planned to do. He had been forced to draw first blood. Now he had the fearsome task of making sure the next blood spilt in the war wasn't his, on territory in which he was completely lost. His only edge, sneakiness of movement and surprise in attack, had been lost.

'Don't you try and go for your gun, mister,' he said, 'or there'll be more blood spilt, lots of it, all yours. Just get your buddy up on his horse and get back to your boss. Tell him to give up his crazy idea of wanting to be top dog in the valley.'

The ranch hand gimlet-eyed Mike. 'You're dead, boy,' he said, flat-voiced. 'You ain't buried yet but you're dead. The boss will raise a big hunt for you, drag you outa what hole out here you're hidin' in. Let's go, Curly, and get those wounds of yours seen to and let that asshole say his prayers.' He hard-eyed

Billy Jayhawk. 'And you as well, Billy, if part-Injuns say their prayers, because you'll swing for real the next time.' He turned his back on Mike and helped his partner to get into his saddle, the wounded man groaning and dirty-mouthing Mike as he heaved himself up on to his horse.

Mike kept the shotgun trained on the pair until all he could see of them was their trail dust, then he took a look at the man he had saved from a hanging as he struggled to his feet with his hands bound behind his back, to find he wasn't a man but a kid no older than he was, a scrawny, lean-faced kid dressed in a ragbag of clothes even a New York bum would be too proud to be seen walking around in.

'You should have killed him,' Billy Jayhawk said. 'It would'uv been one less to kill next time round. Now I'd be obliged if you could cut these god-damned ropes and let me get to hell far away from here. And you'd be sensible to do likewise.' Billy grinned at Mike.

'And thanks for saving me from an early grave.'

In spite of his smile and thank you, Billy was wondering just who his rescuer was and why he had stuck his neck out to save a ragged-ass 'breed from a hanging. He didn't look old enough, or handle a gun expertly enough to be an experienced lawman. He could be a kid down on his luck trying to earn himself some cash by being a bounty hunter. Could have saved him, Billy thought, uneasily, to hand him over to one of the other ranchers in the valley for the price on his head. Slade wasn't the only rancher in the territory who wanted to see him strung up for cattle-lifting.

Mike, mind still occupied with the dangerous situation he was in, cut Billy Jayhawk's bonds with the knife he had picked up off the ground.

'Thanks again, friend,' Billy said, rubbing his wrists to restore the circulation. 'Another coupla minutes and you'd be diggin' a hole for me.' He grinned. 'I'll have my knife back, then, as I said, we oughta get someplace else, fast.'

Mike handed Billy his knife and Billy's grin switched off as, with a flick of his wrist, he held the blade under his saviour's chin. 'Now tell me who you are, mister,' he growled. 'I ain't about to exchange one cattleman's rope for another cowman's noose.'

Mike saw red. He had landed himself up to the eyeballs in real trouble to save the scrawny kid's life and now the ungrateful son-of-a-bitch was threatening him. Heedless of the knife's closeness to his throat Mike reacted to the deadly threat by swaying to his left as a boxer would do to dodge an opponent's blow, at the same time his right fist flashed out in a powerful jab.

Billy heard bells ringing in his ears and saw flashing bright lights, then everything went black for him as he crumpled at the knees and hit the ground again, the knife falling out of his hand. In a minute or two later, when he came to, feeling as though every tooth in his head had been rattled loose, his rescuer was standing over him, with his shotgun pressed hard against his chest.

'You ragged-assed, double-timin' bastard!' Mike yelled, glaring-eyed, shotgun held in arms that trembled with barely controlled anger. 'I've landed myself right in the shit saving your dirty neck. Try any more tricks and I'll let you have both barrels. I've got myself worked up into a mood I ain't experienced before, a real nasty mood.' He stepped back from Billy. 'Now, get up nice and easy-like and get to hell outa my sight, or you could end up bein' the second man I've killed.'

'The second man you've killed?' repeated a surprised Billy, as he heaved himself upright. 'Ain't you a lawman then?'

'Me, a lawman?' Mike's laugh lacked humour. 'I'm wanted for a so-called murder in San Francisco,' he said. 'I'm headin' East to escape any lawmen who could be tryin' to arrest me. Then, back there in Mile Creek, I helped a coupla sheepherders who were havin' trouble with a roughneck and got myself caught up in the war this fella Slade has sicked on the sheepherders. I'm out here to stir things up somewhat for Slade.'

Mike didn't tell Billy that one of the sheepherders he had helped out was a pretty young girl, or he could think he was crazy risking his life to win the favours of a girl he had only known for a few hours.

Billy already knew the man he tagged as an Easterner by the way he spoke, was crazy and, like old Valdez had opined, it would only be a matter of time before his foolishness cost him his life. Taking on the hard men who rode for Slade, who would soon be riding out with blood in their eyes to avenge the wounding of one of their own, was as crazy as anything he had heard of. Almost as loco as he was living his life one jump ahead of a cattleman's hanging party. Billy kept his thoughts to himself, not wanting to upset the young dude more than he'd already done by calling him a crazy fool.

'I'm sorry I held my knife agin you,' he said, apologetically. 'But when a fella's been as close to departin' this sweet earth as I've just been he ends up kinda nervous. Bein' that every cattle owner in the territory is itchin' to string me up I thought you saved my neck so you could hand me over to one of them and claim the bounty they've got on my head. You'll get no more trouble from me, friend.' He smiled and stuck out his hand. 'Shake; you have Billy Jayhawk's word on it.'

Billy matched his smile and gripped the offered hand. 'I'll accept your word, Mr Jayhawk,' he said. 'I'm Mike Tilman, late of New York City.'

'I'm part Paiute, on my ma's side,' Billy said. 'So I know all about fellas attemptin' things they've got the strong urge to carry out. Full-bloods call it their destiny; it's what's written down in their Book of Life the way things are goin' for them.' Then Billy thought he should warn Mike just what odds he was facing. 'But that don't mean they rode out mad-assed into a hairy situation, especially when the odds are stacked high agin them followin' their so-called fate.'

'You tryin' to tell me I'm takin' on more than I can handle, Mr Jayhawk?' Mike said stiffly, his pride ruffled. 'I damn well know that!' He thin-smiled. 'And I ain't shortened the odds any by comin' out into the open to save your life. My plan was to sneak in on Slade when it got dark and try and poke him in the eye with a stick, as we say back in the Bronx.'

'Yeah, I can see how I spoilt your grand plan, Mr Tilson,' replied Billy. 'But if you had let those bastards string me up and carried on with your sneakin'-around plan you would have only been puttin' your death off by a few hours.' Billy laughed at Mike's puzzled look. 'You ain't sneakin' around at all, friend, you're leavin' a trail a one-eyed drunk could pick up. Slade has men prowlin' all across his range lookin' for signs of any riders comin' on to his land. They'll have you kickin' on the end of a rope, or pumped full of lead in no time at all.'

Mike knew what Billy Jayhawk had said was right, though he had hoped he could have got at least one good strike against Slade before the worst happened to him. Now it looked as if he wouldn't get that way-out chance. Stubborn-jawed he said, 'Well I'll just have to see how things go, won't I? I sure ain't a quitter.'

And neither was he, Billy thought, soberly, and his own bull-headed pride had almost got him strung up. He came to a sudden and surprising decision. Straight-eying Mike he said, 'If you want a pard, Mike, to help you push that stick in Slade's eye, I'm willin' to be that *hombre*. I owe the sonuvabitch a jab or two for what his boys tried to do with me.' He grinned. 'And I ain't speakin' fork-tongued like most of you white-eyes speak.'

Mike didn't hesitate one second in

accepting Billy Jayhawk's offer of being his partner. The part-Indian had made him realize his half-baked plan was even madder than he had thought. He grinned, his cockiness returning. 'What chance has Slade and his bully boys got takin' on half-Injun and half-Irish hell raisers.'

'No chance at all, pard,' replied Billy, straight-faced. He bent down and picked up his knife and slipped it down the top of his right boot. Then he took hold of his pistol belt lying on the ground beside his horse, buckled it about his waist and in one flying leap was sitting in his saddle.

'We'll use the crick to hide our tracks, Mike,' he said. 'Come out of the water where those cows have been tramplin' over. That oughta cut off our tracks dead to anyone but an Indian. Then I'll call on my ma's blood to find us a place to hole-up safely till it's time to pay a call on Mr High-and-Mighty Slade.'

★ ★ ★

Slade got up from his chair and strode up and down behind his desk like some caged wildcat. He couldn't believe what he had heard from Simpson. His straw boss had come bursting into his den with the disturbing news that a kid had got the drop on Curly and Les when they were about to string up the cattle-lifting 'breed, Billy Jayhawk, Curly coming in with a load of buckshot in his legs.

What the hell was going on? Slade thought angrily. All he was getting was bad news and he was paying men good money to make sure things were going his way. First the gunslinger Bannister was in the territory working for the opposition; then Mel and Jake not returning from their last raid on the C L line cabins, and now Curly, wounded.

Slade stopped his wild pacing and hard-eyed his straw boss. 'You're telling me,' he snarled, 'that those apologies for ranch hands allowed a kid to throw down on them? Who is he? Does he work alongside Bannister? Is he responsible for Mel and Jake not showing up?'

'I don't know, boss,' replied Simpson. 'Cassidy reckons it could be the same kid who beat up Lovell and he's linked with the sheepherders. I figure him and the 'breed are with the sheepherders right now.'

'With the sheepherders, eh,' Slade growled. His eyes narrowed in pinpoints of hate. 'Their days of tending sheep in the valley have just come to an end. Cassidy and Peckham are intending to pay a visit to that shanty town to put this mysterious kid in his place, a shallow hole in the ground. Have them ride there in the morning and take some of the crew with them and hit those sheepmen real hard.'

10

Wendell dropped slowly on to his knees, pistol held out in front of him on hearing the chink of iron striking against rock in the darkness away to his left, the sound of an approaching rider. He knew he was taking a big risk carrying the war against Slade right up to the rancher's front door but he didn't want the trouble he was being paid to settle to drag into a long struggle with the rancher's men doing most of the bloodletting.

He had evened up the score slightly by his shooting of the two Double X killers and now he wanted Slade to taste some of the bitter medicine he was dishing out to the men who were resisting his attempts to take over all the grass and water in the valley.

He sank lower to the ground as he picked out the dim, bulky shape of a horse and rider silhouetted against the backdrop of a starlit sky. Wendell eased back the hammer of the Colt and waited, nerves taut as the rider passed across his front, close enough for him to smell the tangy sweat of the horse and the smoke from the guard's red-tipped makings.

If he was spotted and had to shoot down the guard he would have to high-tail it back to his horse tethered more than half a mile behind him, hoping the darkness would allow him to slip between the other mounted guards who must be prowling about this close to the ranch big house and would be fully alerted by the sound of a pistol shot. Then there was the added danger of breaking his neck over some obstacle in the dark, or breaking a leg, which would be just as fatal, lying there unable to move, living as long as it took him to fire off all his reloads.

Wendell breathed a silent but deep sigh of relief as the guard disappeared into the night showing no signs of alarm. He listened for several minutes, the sweat ice-cold on his brow, until he was satisfied the danger had passed. He got to his feet to move forward in a crouching walk, as noiseless and speedily as an Indian.

*   *   *

Mike waited anxiously for Billy Jayhawk's return. He was lying in a patch of long dew-wet grass, the dampness penetrating right through to his skin. Raising his head slightly he could see the well-lit front porch of Slade's ranch house, and the guard sitting outside the front door. The rest of the building, what Billy had called the big house, was in darkness.

Billy had gone crawling somewhere up ahead to see if they could make it to the large barn close enough to the house to catch the light from the lamps on the porch without been seen by the guard. Mike would have liked to put a torch to Slade's fine house but that would have been too risky an undertaking. Pushing their present good fortune too far. So, on Billy Jayhawk's advice, he had settled for burning down the barn.

Good fortune, luck, whatever, he knew had nothing to do with the pair of them getting within striking distance of poking Slade in the eyes. It was all down to Billy Jayhawk's inherited tracking skills.

They had come out of the creek and rode along the well-churned-up ground of the broad trail the cattle had made coming to the water. They had holed-up until dark in a brush-ringed hollow, a slight dip that Mike didn't think it possible to hide a man in, let alone two men and their mounts, but Billy had thought otherwise and he was in no position to question his say-so.

As soon as the light had gone from the land, Billy had said it was time to start their small war against Slade. 'We go in Injun-style,' he told Mike. 'Sneak in on foot. Stay close to me, and if I drop to the ground you do likewise, quickly, OK?'

'OK? You're the boss,' replied Mike. He had taken a look at the featureless blackness outside their hole-up that they would have to negotiate. Damn right he would stay close to his pard, he thought. Twenty yards out in the darkness from where he was standing on his ownsome he would be lucky to stumble his way back to the horses. He would never again doubt his partner's skill in smelling his way around in the dark. And that's all it could be, smelling, for Mike reckoned his eyesight was as keen as Billy's, yet he hadn't seen the night rider until his horse had practically stepped on his face minutes after Billy had dragged him to the ground.

$$\star \quad \star \quad \star$$

Wendell quietly elbowed his way through the grass closing in on the man lying on the ground in front of him.

From his worm's-eye view, having dropped to the ground since he had seen the mounted guard and kept low, he had picked out the dark, bulky shape of what could only be a man lying doggo. Who he was had Wendell puzzled. If he was a Double X man why was he lying there facing the ranch house and not outwards looking for anyone likely to be a threat against the Double X? It didn't matter who the man was, he thought, the watcher had to be put out of action. He wanted a clear way out when he set fire to Slade's house. Wendell drew out his pistol ready to cold-cock the man who could be a danger to him when it was time to cut and run for it.

Mike's nerves twitched on hearing a slight rustling behind him. He twisted round, hissing nervously, 'Is that you, Billy?'

Wendell gasped in surprise, holding his knees-and-elbows crawl, answering Mike's question with one of his own. 'Is that the New York kid?' he said, still holding his pistol high to bring it sweeping down for the KO blow just in case he had heard wrong.

It was Mike's turn to gasp. 'Mr Bannister! You almost scared the crap outa me! What the hell are you doin' here?'

Wendell grinned. 'I could ask why a city dude kid is risking being shot prowling about on Double X land. I — ' Wendell's voice dried up and his smile became a rictus grimace, as a knife point pricked at the back of his neck. He cursed, silently. He had crawled his way into an ambush.

'Is this fella a friend of yours, Mike?' Billy Jayhawk said. 'If he ain't, I'm itchin' to get me my first scalp, a white-eyes at that.'

'He's OK, Billy Jayhawk!' Mike said frantically. 'He's a gunfighter, a Mr Bannister, a friend of mine.'

Billy slipped his knife back into his boot. Thankfully, Wendell turned to his side to see who it was who had caught him unawares, a part-Indian by the sound of his name. Jesus, Wendell thought, another youngster. Then told himself he must be getting too old for this regulating business when two kids could outwit him.

'You ain't one of Slade's crew then?' Billy said.

'No I'm not,' replied Wendell, eager to put Billy Jayhawk at ease. Part-Indian men, he knew, were hot-tempered, tetchy *hombres*. 'I've been hired to fight Slade.' Then he asked, 'Would you have carried out your threat, scalped me, Mr Jayhawk?'

Billy's teeth gleamed white in the dark in a face-splitting grin. 'Now we'll never know, white-eye, will we?'

Not wanting to show the 'breed kid that a white-eye could be scared easily, Wendell managed a smile. 'You could have done so, Mr Jayhawk,' he said. 'You had all the edge. Now, we're all *amigos* and we're here for the same reason, to put a fire under Slade's ass. I reckon we should discuss how that should be done, pronto, before any night riders swing by this way again.'

'Billy thinks the ranch house is too well lit for us to get close enough to set fire to it without that guard spottin' us,' Mike said. 'He's been checkin' out that big barn to see if it's safe enough to start a fire there.'

Wendell took his first close look at the ranch house. 'It was also my intention to torch it, but I'd have to agree with Mr Jayhawk's considered opinion; it's too risky. We could make it there though we'd be lucky to get back to our horses without being shot down. The barn it will have to be.'

'It'll be no problem at all burnin' that place down, Mr Bannister,' Billy Jayhawk said. 'It's full of bales of hay, a small fire in there will smoulder long enough for the three of us to be gone from here before the flames take hold and are seen. There's loose planks on the farside wall so there'll be no trouble for whoever of us is going inside to light the match unseen.' Billy grinned again. 'I don't want to boast, pards,' he said.

'But that ain't a job for clumsy-footed white-eyes.'

'You'll get no disagreement from me on that suggestion, Mr Jayhawk,' Wendell said. 'Me and Mr Tilman will cover you.'

'I'll try not to scare you both when I come back,' Billy said, straight-faced, and slipped from Wendell's side as silently as he had come on to him with the knife in his hand.

Wendell unslung his rifle from his back. 'Let's play our part in this shindig, Mr Tilman,' he said, and drew a bead on the guard on the porch. 'Have you a rifle?'

'No,' replied Mike. 'As you know I ain't fired one in the daylight yet, Mr Bannister. I can't see me doin' any good firin' one at night. I've got one of these, just like yours.' He showed Wendell the sawn-off shotgun. 'Even a dude like me can hit what he's aimin' at, if he's close enough to it.'

'It isn't much use against that fella squatting on the porch, Mr Tilman,'

Wendell said. 'If that guard gets up off his ass and makes a dash for the barn I'll bring him down, then you and me get to hell out of here fast and back to our horses. We're in no position to take on the Double X wild boys. Mr Jayhawk, I don't doubt, will be able to fend for himself. By the way, Mr Tilman, how did you meet up with our part-Indian *compadre* and end up here, burning down Slade's barn? I thought you were tryin' to get back to New York?'

'Yeah, that was my intention, Mr Bannister,' replied Mike. 'But things don't always run the way you want them to, and I found myself takin' sides with the sheepherders in their fight against that bullyin' bastard in yonder house.'

Wendell half-smiled. He had more than an inkling the pretty young girl the kid had helped out back in Mile Creek was the reason he wasn't trailing eastwards. Though it was none of his business to poke his nose into Mr

142

Tilman's private affairs.

'I saved Billy Jayhawk from a hangin', Mr Bannister,' Mike continued. 'Two of Slade's men were about to string him up. I had to shoot one of them in the legs. Then both of us, bein' no lovers of Mr Slade, it seemed natural for me and Billy to be partners in the fight. Especially when I ain't much good wanderin' about on all this grass on my own. I ain't no general, Mr Bannister, but I know enough about fightin' — the back alley sort — that the more there are of you the better the chances of your side comin' out the winner. I told Mr Millar, Kath's father — Kath is the name of the girl with the wagon in Mile Creek — that the only way the sheepmen could beat off Slade was to join up with the ranchers Slade was also tryin' to drive off their land. He said sheepmen and cowmen don't hit it off together. I couldn't sit on my ass doin' damn all, not the way I feel towards Kath.' Mike's face twisted in an angry scowl. 'On my own territory, Mr

Bannister, I never allow any asshole to harass me, or my friends, without fightin' back. So, crazy or not, here I am.'

Wendell knew he was in no position to question the craziness or otherwise of the kid's action, he was every bit as loco hiring himself out as a troubleshooter. Mike, a born firebrand, a man who would pick himself up, no matter how many times he had been knocked down in a fight, and toe the line, was putting his life in jeopardy for the affections of a girl he had just met. Only this fight was with guns and a man shot full of lead was in no position to get back up on to his feet.

And what Mike had said about the sheepherders allying themselves with Al Brown and the rest of the small ranchers threatened by Slade's plan for the valley made sense. Any other thoughts Wendell might have had concerning the war against Slade were cut short when Billy Jayhawk, in true

Indian-style suddenly appeared at his side.

'Mr Jayhawk,' Wendell said. 'You don't need your big knife to scare a fella half to death, the way you have of sneaking up on him does just as well.' Face serious he said, 'How did it go?'

Billy grinned. 'It's time we were makin' ourselves scarce, Mr Bannister,' he said. 'In about ten, fifteen minutes time, Mr Slade is goin' to lose a whole heap of winter fodder, and one fine barn.'

'If you boys are going back to the sheepherders' settlement,' Wendell said, 'I'll go with you. M'be if I sweet-talk the sheep men they'll agree to fight alongside the man who's hired me. That's if I can persuade Al Brown sheepmen ain't as low life as sodbusters, and that there should be enough grass and water in the valley for both sheep and cows once Slade's cut down to size. Explain to him that he and the other small owners need all the allies they can get, for when Slade sees

145

his barn going up in smoke and flames he'll be as mad as hell and will really hot up his war.'

* * *

From his front porch, a stone-faced Slade watched his crew's frantic but futile attempts to extinguish the fire in the barn, the men having to pull back for their safety as the flames whipped by the strong night wind took hold of the tarred roof.

A smoke-blackened, exhausted Simpson came up on to the porch. 'It's no good, Mr Slade,' he said. 'The fire's got too big a hold. I'll have some of the boys dampen down this roof just in case the wind changes and blows sparks this way.'

'So it looks as though that Eastern kid and the 'breed didn't ride off my range after shootin' Curly,' Slade grated, fish-eyeing his straw boss. 'The sonsuvbitches outfoxed us.'

Simpson looked out into the night,

wary-eyed, uneasy, wondering if the two fire-raisers were out there about to start another blaze.

'Let the goddamned barn burn, Simpson,' Slade said. 'And get half the crew saddled up, pronto. Get them to cut out a coupla hundred cows from the herd, and pay that call on the sheepherders a few hours earlier. I'm finished pussy-footin' it around. I can't be blamed if a bunch of Double X cows takes off in a night stampede and smashes some sheepherders' homes into kindlin', not when my boys are out tryin' to turn 'em. If that kid and the 'breed are at the settlement tell Cassidy I want them alive and brought back here so I can hang them personally, understand?'

'Understood, boss,' replied Simpson, grinning wild-eyed. 'It'll be a downright shame that we couldn't stop the longhorns from causin' all that damage.' He stepped down from the porch and began shouting out orders.

The barn-burners rode fast along the ridge leading to the escape route through the hills. Behind them they could see a flickering red glow reflected in the night sky.

Wendell smiled. 'That sight must set your Indian blood racing, Mr Jayhawk,' he said. 'Seeing a white-eye's barn burning by your hand.'

'It kinda pleases my white-eye blood as well, Mr Bannister,' replied Billy. 'Even things up somewhat for those two bastards who work for Slade half-chokin' me to death.'

Once off the flat and into the hills Billy called a halt. 'I ain't got enough 'Ute blood in me to lead you back to the sheepherders' settlement without riskin' breakin' the horses' legs. I figure we should hole up here till first light. If it's OK with you white-eyes.'

'It's OK by me, Billy,' Mike said. 'I ain't sure I could find my way there in daylight unless the trail was sign-posted. And, besides, I could do with gettin' off this horse for a spell. I ain't got a leather-ass yet like you two fellas. What say you, Mr Bannister?'

'It's been your party, boys,' replied Wendell. 'I'm just tagging along for the fun. Resting up here is OK by me.'

11

Kath stood on the porch still in her night clothes, unable to sleep for worrying about Mike — a city boy out on the plains on his own, probably being hunted down by Slade's bully boys.

At first she had thought Mike had left the settlement to continue his journey back to New York. Which was natural, she told herself, for a boy raised in the biggest, finest city in the whole of America, wouldn't think much of how the sheepherders lived and would want to quit the settlement as soon as he could. Kath remembered how unimpressed he was on first seeing the settlement. Yet she was angry, and disappointed, with Mike for not having the decency to say his goodbyes to her and her folk. And she had foolishly believed he had been fond of her.

On hearing from Señor Valdez the reason why Mike had left the settlement she had still been angry with him, and worried sick at his dangerous foolhardiness at risking his life for folk he hardly knew, though, at the same time, flattered and proud knowing somehow Mike was putting his life on the line mainly for her sake.

'He'll be OK, Señorita Millar,' Valdez said, mentally crossing himself for uttering such a brazen lie. He firmly believed the young *hombre* was already dead, shot down by the Double X ranch hands.

'I pray so, Señor Valdez, I pray so,' Kath said, tears coursing down her cheeks, as she ran indoors to tell her parents that the boy she had strong feelings for hadn't acted ungratefully.

Kath heard a distant rumble of what she took to be thunder and she thought of the discomfort Mike must be suffering caught on the open plain by a whiplashing rain-storm. Valdez heard the 'thunder', but sleeping in a tent with only a blanket between him and the ground he felt the earth vibrating beneath him. His blood froze. The rumbling was man made! The gringo son-of-a-bitch, Slade, was sending his cattle to clear the sheepherders from the valleys. Cursing, grabbing his rifle, he stumbled out of his tent.

His rapid rifle discharges in the night sky and wild shouting brought Kath fully awake, thinking for a few seconds the old Mexican had got himself drunk on some of the whiskey he had brought back with the supplies they had picked up at Mile Creek. Then her face whitened in terror as she realized what she had thought was thunder was the drumming of hundreds of longhorn hoofs pounding down the valley towards the settlement. She turned and ran back into the shack yelling hysterically to wake up her father and mother.

In the panic-stricken chaos treasured family possessions had to be left, the saving of lives coming first. Men with pants hanging round their knees, shirt-tails flying, men only wearing long woolly underpants, women in their night clothes, some unashamedly showing their drawers, carried or dragged their frightened children, many crying at being dragged from their warm beds, to the safety of the high ground on the other side of the creek. The sheep had to fend for themselves, scattering which way and every way as the first of the wild-eyed, bellowing herd came on the settlement with the ferocity of a tidal wave.

Simpson had to try hard to keep the satisfied smirk off his face. The settlement looked as though a Kansas twister had whirled its way through it. Shacks were leaning lopsidedly, shacks with porches trampled to kindling, tent tarps ripped to shreds by sharp hoofs. The mangled dead sheep lay in their scores on the ground and in the creek. Mr Slade, Simpson opined, would be highly pleased.

Then he looked at the sheepherders

153

and their families and his grin almost burst through. White-faced with cold and shock, half-naked, they picked over the the shattered ruins of what a few hours ago had been their homes, for anything worth saving to get them through the next night in the open. Soon, Simpson reckoned, the dead sheep would have to be burnt or the whole place would stink and that would bring disease and the winged and four-legged scavengers here. All in all, he thought, the sheepherders had the appearance of folk ready to quit raising sheep in the valley and pull out. And the only way they could do that was to walk out, as the three wagons they regularly used to haul in supplies were lying on their sides, smashed to pieces.

Simpson leant across his saddle and spoke to the man he knew to be the spokesman of the sheepmen, who along with his wife and daughter, was trying to clear a way through a broken porch so they could get into their shack, the rear of it having caved in. Forked-tongued he said, 'I'm real sorry, Mr Millar, about all this mess; my boys tried their best to swing the stampede away from your homes, but you know how it is with spooked longhorns, the crazy critters race like hell in the direction they want to go 'till they run outa steam.'

Jason Millar knew how it was all right, and not the way Simpson was telling it. That son-of-a-bitch Slade had finally decided to clear them out of the valley and make it seem like an act of God, a unpreventable stampede. He looked up at Slade's straw boss with burning hate in his eyes. Unarmed, he could do nothing. If he'd had his rifle he was mad enough to blow Simpson clear out of his saddle. Accusing Simpson of lying would just be a waste of breath.

Supposing he'd had his rifle and given in to his mad rage and shot Simpson, Slade's two hired guns, up on horses behind Simpson, would have gunned him down. Ma and Kath had enough grief to bear right now, losing most of what they owned, without seeing him stretched out dead on the ground.

'I can't see that Eastern kid hangin' around here,' Simpson said. 'We're lookin' for him and that thievin' 'breed, Billy Jayhawk. The pair of them burnt down Mr Slade's big barn last night. He intends hangin' them.' He twisted round in his saddle. 'You two boys stay here in case the pair show up later.' He hard-eyed Cassidy and Peckham. 'Remember, Mr Slade wants them alive. I'll go and see if the longhorns have run themselves into the ground.'

Cassidy grinned. 'He'll get them alive, Simpson. Though that don't mean me and Peckham won't shoot lumps out the Eastern kid for what he did to Lovell.'

Jason watched Simpson ride away, his spirits lifted slightly. Mr Tilman had struck a blow against Slade for them. Now he could understand the reason for the so-called accidental stampede. Still, he thought, he wouldn't hold that against the boy. Slade had only made his move to clear them out of the valley sooner than he had probably intended to. At least they had got one blow against Slade, burning down his barn, hurting the prodding man's pride somewhat. Jason wondered how Mr Tilman had met up with the young 'breed, Billy Jayhawk, a posted outlaw wanted for sheep-stealing as well as cattle-lifting.

Now another worry was chewing away at Jason's guts, the urgency to warn Mr Tilman and his partner of the trap they were riding into if they came back to the settlement. His wife and daughter had managed to force their way into the house while Simpson had been talking to him and were busy changing out of their night clothes when he walked in on them.

'Mr Tilman's still alive, Kath,' he said. 'According to Simpson, the boy and Billy Jayhawk set fire to one of

Slade's barns last night. The bad news is that those two hired guns with Simpson are staying here ready to jump them if they head back this way. We've got to warn them somehow what's waiting for them here.'

'I'll warn him, Pa,' Kath said without any hesitation, her face lighting up, hardly believing the much-prayed-for news that Mike was safe and well. 'I'll go by the old path through the brush on the other side of the creek. Those two men on the north ridge won't catch a glimpse of me, I promise. If Mike is riding back here I can stop him on the trail well out of sight of Slade's men.'

Jason shot a questioning glance at his wife. Mrs Millar saw the pleading look on Kath's face. Her daughter, she suddenly realized, was in love with the boy. She came to a decision. 'We can't allow Slade's gunmen get their hands on Mr Tilman, Pa,' she said. 'Not when we know what Slade will do to him. Let Kath go,' she said. 'But you take care, girl; those men are hired killers, understand?'

'You go then, Kath,' Jason said reluctantly. 'But do as your ma said, take care.' He wasn't happy at Kath putting her life at risk. If things went badly wrong and it came to a gunfight between the two boys and the hired guns, Kath could be in the middle of it and could end up getting herself shot. In spite of his fears, Jason knew Kath had the better chance of sneaking out of the settlement than he had. The two gunmen would be watching him and the rest of the men like hawks in case of trouble breaking out.

Kath was in such a high state of excitement at the prospect of meeting Mike again she didn't care if the men were cold-blooded killers or not. Saving the boy she had fallen in love with came before her personal safety. She smiled reassuringly at her parents. 'I'll take care, I promise.' She left them both wondering and worrying if they had made the right decision.

12

At daybreak, they broke camp and Billy Jayhawk led his two *compadres* through the trails and tracks in the hills, to well south of the settlement before cutting back into the valley again. Then he headed north to the settlement. Billy was taking no chances of leading Mike and Mr Bannister into an ambush. He had kept his own skin safe since the day he had lifted his first maverick by always outsmarting the ranchers from whom he had stolen cattle.

By now, Slade would have guessed that one of the men who had set fire to his barn had links with the sheepherders and it would be an obvious move on his part to have men watching the trails leading to the settlement on the off chance of catching the fire raisers sneaking back there, or leaving the settlement to inflict more damage to

Double X property. Billy was taking his partners the long way round, but it could turn out to be the safest route for them.

Closing in on the settlement they came across the first of the trampled-to-death sheep. 'Sweet Jesus!' Mike gasped. 'There's hundreds of them. Have they been poisoned, Mr Bannister?'

Wendell's face stoned over. 'Not poisoned, Mr Tilman,' he replied. 'Just the results of Slade's calling cards. Burning down his barn must have touched the sonuvabitch on the raw.'

'Calling cards?' asked a puzzled Mike.

'Yeah, in the shape of a bunch of cattle,' Wendell said, grimly, 'Slade has had his boys drive a herd through the settlement, high-tailin' it through. The cows will have flattened not only any sheep in their path but everything else in their way, shacks, people. Is that the way you read it, my Indian friend?' Wendell screwed round in his saddle to face Billy Jayhawk who was bringing up the rear. His eyebrows rose in surprise. His Indian 'friend' had vanished.

He looked back at Mike. 'I'm glad that young hellion is on our side, Mr Tilman,' he said. 'The way he comes and goes gets my scalp tingling.'

'Why has he gone?' Mike said.

Wendell shrugged. 'There's no telling how even a part-Indian acts sometimes. Their so-called spirits tell them things we white-eyes aren't privy to. Let's push on to the settlement and see how the folk there fared. I can't see any dust raised by a herd of long-horns so I reckon the cows have done what they had to do and are now being driven back on to Double X land.'

Following Wendell, Mike kneed his horse into a canter, his face grim, his insides churning over at the dread of what could have happened to Kath and her parents.

Seeing the dead sheep hadn't upset or alarmed Billy Jayhawk any. What worried him was live men, men who would take a delight in shooting him down like some mad dog. His Indian sixth sense was ringing alarm bells in his ears that suchlike men were close by. True, or just his nerves playing him up didn't matter to Billy Jayhawk. He took heed of the warning, not wanting to learn the hard way, a Winchester shell tearing through his flesh, his nerves had been right all along. Without saying a word to his two partners, he pulled his horse's head around and rode down into a nearby gully.

The first of the shattered shacks came in sight, their owners piling undamaged pieces of furniture outside them. Mike's worries about Kath's wellbeing turned to a burning hatred against Slade.

'What manner of asshole would do this to hard-workin' folk, Mr Bannister?' he said, almost snarling out the words. 'Ain't there no law out here?'

'A man cursed with a mean kind of pride,' replied Wendell. 'A twisted sense of pride that wants him to be the boss man in the territory, an uncrowned king so to speak. Texas and New Mexico, so I'm led to believe, has suchlike prodding men, running vast herds of cows on ranges bigger than a state county. They make their own laws and anyone doubting their say-so gets stomped on. Slade hankers to be just as big and powerful. Now you introduce me to the man who these folks listen to then m'be we can get something set up so we can meet Slade on more equal terms.'

★　★　★

'Hey, Valdez, are there any of Slade's men still hangin' around here?'

Valdez, busy dragging his dead stock out of the creek, paused in his soul-destroying chore, wondering if he had heard the soft-voiced question. He could see no one in the brush behind him and a man who had seen his life's work destroyed in a few minutes, and too old to start up again, was entitled to hear voices in his head.

'Are you deaf, old man?' Billy Jayhawk said impatiently. He pushed the brush aside slightly and Valdez caught a glimpse of a hawk-like face.

'*Madre de Dios*!' he breathed. 'Billy Jayhawk!' Valdez knew Billy. Sometimes when he was grazing his sheep on the open plain the 'breed would stop off at his camp for coffee and a handful of tobacco. Being wanted by the cattlemen for stealing their cows made Billy, part Paiute or not, a friend of the sheepherders. 'You are in great danger, Billy,' he said. 'Two of Slade's pistoleros are on the ridge, hoping to catch you and the young *hombre*. That dog, Slade, was angry at you two for burning down his barn so he sent his cattle here to destroy our homes as revenge.' Valdez looked over his shoulder to see if Billy was hearing what he was telling him, and found out he was talking to the patch of brush. Billy had had his uneasiness justified, and was about to act on it.

Valdez grinned. After Slade's long-horns' fearful night's work he thought he would never smile again. Now he was getting a good feeling Billy and the *hombre* were about to cause Slade to be upset again. Valdez would wager the few live sheep he had left that the rancher would soon lose his two hired pistole-ros.

Cassidy brought the army glasses up to his eyes as he saw two riders approaching the far end of the settle-ment. He knew they couldn't be two of Slade's crew, they were driving the herd back to the Double X range.

'We're back in business, Peckham,' he said. 'A young kid and Mr Wendell Bannister are ridin' in. I never tagged Bannister as a sheep-lover. I thought he was hired by the cattlemen north of Slade's range.' Cassidy's lips parted in a all-tooth, merciless grin. 'I'm gettin' the chance to cut the mean sonuvabitch down to size sooner than I expected.'

'Is the stinkin' 'breed with them?' Peckham asked.

Cassidy lowered the glasses. 'I can't see him, but that part-Injun is a loner; he could be anywhere by now. You keep an eye out for him, Peckham, while I go down and surprise that famous pistolero. Keep a bead on him till I've got him off his horse and disarmed. You have my permission to shoot him dead if he tries to throw down on me. Slade won't be put out if we kill him. It's only the kids he wanted alive.'

For a man of his bulk Cassidy moved swiftly and silently down the grade. His inner fear of knowing he was taking on a man whose rep he envied, a man who would shoot him in the blink of an eye if he saw merely a glimpse of him, gave Cassidy the extra skill to come through the brush without any giveaway shake of a branch.

'Oh my God!' Mrs Millar gasped, hand flying to her mouth. 'Here's Mike, Jason!'

Jason turned and saw the two riders. He swore. Kath was risking her life for nothing. The boy, and whoever it was with him, were riding blindly into the gunmen's trap. He dropped the chair he was holding and made to run down the trail to warn them of their danger and to hell with the Slade's killers on the ridge.

'You just stay put, sheepman,' Cassidy said, standing grinning at Jason from the hidden side of the shack. 'Or that lady wife of yours will be a widow woman. Both of you get back here outa sight, pronto.' Cassidy's grin became a full-blooded laugh. 'I know what's passin' through your mind, sheepman,' he said. 'If I fire at you the shot will warn those two they're ridin' into trouble. But before they can swing their horses' heads round to high-tail it back along the trail, my buddy, up on that ridge, will clear them outa their saddles as easy as I can plug you. So you'll be makin' a widow of your wife for damn all. And you'll be disappointin' me because I want to shoot that fella wearin' the duster.' Cassidy jerked his rifle threateningly at them. 'Now move!' he snarled.

Jason's shoulders sagged. With a look of defeat on his face he said, 'Let's do as he says, Ma.' He took hold of his wife's arm and led her to the rear of the shack.

Cassidy stepped clear of the shack, almost making both horses rear in fright at his sudden appearance. His rifle was aimed at Wendell, his greatest known danger. If Bannister saw as much as an inkling of a chance he would go for it.

'Don't even think about riskin' takin' me on, Bannister,' he said. 'Peckham's back there on the ridge holdin' his Winchester right on you, and I figure you know he's more than a fair shot with a long gun. Between us, I reckon we can put you down for keeps. Now, both of you, just step down nice and easy and unbuckle your gunbelts, then we can go and make a call on Mr Slade.' Cassidy grinned at Mike. 'He'll be real pleased to see you, kid, he's aimin' to string you up.'

Wendell saw the sun glinting off a rifle barrel on the ridge. Cassidy wasn't grandstanding when he said Peckham was a fair shot with a rifle. He and Mr Tilman would be dead if by some miracle he could yank out his pistol and down Cassidy before the gunman could pull back the trigger of his Winchester.

★   ★   ★

Billy Jayhawk snaked his way along the ridge towards the rifleman. The two hired guns had his partners well and truly by the short hairs. He was hoping to give them a slight chance to fight back by putting the man ahead out of business. He crawled several more feet, then had to stop, all his cover at an end. The next few yards was open, stone-covered ground. Even if he had never been a full-blood Paiute, Billy knew he could never cross that strip of ground without alerting the rifleman that he was about to be attacked. His grand plan of sneaking up close and cold-cocking him was out.

The gunman would have to be killed, and silently. A rifle shot up here would have the man covering his partners pulling off shots as fast as he could work his Winchester lever. Billy had never killed a man before, and even though he knew the gunman was a hired killer, he hesitated to take that step now. Then he began to think through his problem as an Indian would. Would a Paiute warrior cry off killing an enemy if his friends were in danger of losing their lives, he asked himself? Especially when he was beholden to one of them for saving him from being lynched.

Billy's mother's blood won out. With his face twisted into a Paiute killing scowl Billy drew out his knife, balanced it in his hand for a moment or two, then with an overarm swing sent the blade flashing on its deadly way.

Billy's aim was true. The knife buried itself deep into the left side of

Peckham's neck, his life's blood spouting out from the wound thick and dark. Peckham died quiet, only Billy hearing the gurgling, coughing sounds coming from the torn throat as Peckham drowned in his own blood. It took all Billy's self-control not to give vent to a Paiute victory whoop.

'Dismount, Mr Tilman,' said a flat-voiced Wendell. He had lasted longer than most men in his dangerous profession. Not many who hired out their guns ended up as old men sitting on a rocking chair on some front porch. What was bitter gall to Wendell was that soon the talk in the bars in the South-west would be how the pistolero, Wendell Bannister, finally met his end by walking into an ambush like some greenhorn dude.

He was only sorry young Tilman would go down with him; he would never see his New York again. Though the boy had chosen to make war against Slade. As he swung down from his saddle, he said, softly, 'We're not dead

172

yet, *amigo*, let's keep it that way. We may get a break.'

Being pushed into a tight corner sent Mike's Irish blood wild. If Mr Bannister had made a move for his pistol he would have snatched for the shotgun stuffed in his bedroll and backed him up. On hearing Mr Bannister's whispered warning he cooled down somewhat. His temper flared up again when he heard Slade's hired gun say, 'How the hell did you get the better of Lovell, half-pint? You musta caught him while he was on the crapper.'

Wendell saw Mike's face working in anger and flashed him a 'stay cool' glance.

'Come on,' Cassidy ordered. 'Start gettin' those gunbelts off, I ain't waitin' all day. And you, Bannister, take that little scattergun outa your duster pocket, nice and slowly like, and sling it across to me. Then I'll get one of these kind sheepmen to rope you up and sling you across the backs of your horses and take you back to the Double

X.' Then Cassidy saw Wendell smiling back at him.

A man facing death, even a cool hand such as Bannister, had no reason to smile unless he had gone loco. Wendell's action puzzled, and worried him. An unexpected chill of fear swept over him and he risked several darting glances to his left and right for signs of Billy Jayhawk creeping up on him.

Billy realized he had to distract the gunman somehow to give Mr Bannister, the expert pistolero, the slight chance to shoot his way out of the hairy situation he and Mike had ridden into. He couldn't trust himself to shoot the gunman dead with his rifle at this range, and wounding him would be no good, he would still be able to use his rifle and gun down his partners. And time wasn't on his side. Then Billy grinned and got to his feet.

'What the hell are you grinnin' at?' Cassidy snarled, his face a mixture of anger and fear.

'I reckon you've got the shakes,

Cass,' Wendell said, still smiling as he unbuckled his gunbelt. 'You're getting a bad feeling that Billy Jayhawk is close by. He's close by all right, he's up on that ridge. So that means your pard is out cold or dead.'

'You lyin' sonuvabitch, I ain't falling for that old trick!' Cassidy shouted. Though doubt had replaced the anger on his face. 'Now get that gunbelt off!'

'That is young Billy waving his hat at us from that ridge, Mr Tilman,' Wendell said conversationally.

Mike grinned, as he squinted up at the figure on the high ground. 'It sure looks like him, Mr Bannister.'

Billy, more Paiute than white-eye, cupped his hands to his mouth and yelled. The bubbling war whoop echoed down from the ridge and got Billy the reaction from Cassidy he had hoped for. A startled Cassidy instinctively turned his head round to see what was happening behind him, his rifle swinging off Wendell. Wendell took the chance Billy Jayhawk had given him

175

and dropped his gunbelt to the ground though his hand still held on to the pistol. He fired three rapid shots from waist high.

Cassidy never got his head back to face Wendell. He grunted as a spasm of infinite pain racked his body as the three heavy shells smashed into his chest, tearing bloody exit holes in his back. His rifle dropped from fingers that could no longer grip. He staggered back on his heels for several paces before falling to the ground, as dead as Peckham.

A drawn-faced, shaky-legged Mike also felt like dropping to the ground. He was finding out it was going to take some time before he got used to how fast and bloodily situations changed in the West. One second a man could be alive and crowing, the next, a blood-oozing corpse. Kath's ma and pa running towards them focused his mind on his earlier worries, was Kath OK?

It seemed to Kath she had been waiting hours at the side of the trail.

Lying under a sheltering patch of brush she was sweaty, itchy and thirsty. And the worry she was feeling for Mike clawed like bile at the back of her throat. The faint sounding of gunshots from the direction of the settlement had her leaping to her feet crying out in alarm, the rough twigs drawing blood on her face and arms. Then, sobbing, she set off running back along the trail to the settlement, trying not to think of the fearful scene, Mike lying dead, waiting for her there.

'Is Kath OK, Mr Millar,' Mike blurted out, when the Millars came up to him.

Jason smiled. 'She's all right, Mike,' he replied. 'She took it in her head to go so far along the north trail to warn you what was waiting for you here if you showed up.'

A much relieved Mike introduced Wendell and Billy Jayhawk to the Millars and the few sheepherders who had gathered around them. Billy was looking as pleased as a young Paiute buck claiming his first scalp.

'Ain't you the hired gun who works for the cattlemen?' one of the sheepherders asked, looking suspicious-eyed at Wendell. Mike, still nervy at his close brush with death, and worrying about Kath out there on the plains on her own, snapped at the questioner before Wendell could answer him.

'Mr Bannister is fightin' for you sheepherders now! That fella lyin' there proves it, I reckon.' He wanted to add that Mr Bannister was doing the job they should be doing, shooting down Slade's men, though not wanting a falling-out with the parents of the girl he had fallen in love with, he held his peace.

'The rancher I regulate for,' Wendell said, 'has no dispute with you sheepmen.' Wendell thin-smiled. 'That don't mean he's full of brotherly love for you, but I give you my word he's not putting himself out to clear you from the valley the way Slade's trying to do. The question is what are you folk going to do? Quit your homes and land, give Slade what he craves for, or are you going to join up with the cattleman I work for and take the fight to Slade? Neither you or the crews on the northern ranches are strong enough on your own to take part in a full-scale war with Slade.' He smiled at Mike and Billy Jayhawk. 'These young hellions here are doing their own style of fighting Slade. They were either brave or crazy enough to burn down Slade's big barn. They were intending to burn down the ranch house, but they had the wisdom not to bite off more than they could chew.'

'Yeah, we know that piece of news,' the sheepman who had challenged Wendell said sourly. He waved his hand at the destruction around him. 'This is Slade's reaction. I've lost my home, my sheep, everything!'

'We've all lost a great deal, Will,' Mr Millar said. 'What's done is done, it can't be altered. If Slade hadn't sent his longhorns in last night he would have done so tomorrow, or the next night. We all knew that, we've been living on borrowed time. It's as Mr Bannister said, what do we do now? I've had a bellyful of Slade's prodding, I aim to fight him. If there's other men in the settlement think as I do ask them to meet me in my house.' Jason half-smiled. 'Or what's left standing of it.'

The sheepherders broke up to pass Jason's message around the settlement. Jason looked at Wendell. 'You'll get your men, Mr Bannister,' he said, 'Never fear. You can push men till some of them break, but some find the strength, or the hate, to fight back. Slade will soon find out we sheepherders ain't the quitting kind.' Jason pointed at Cassidy's body. 'What about him, and that other fella up on the ridge?'

'You and your good lady get back to your home, Mr Millar,' Wendell said. 'Me and the boys will dispose of the bodies then join you later to discuss tactics on how we can hit back at Slade.'

'Aren't you goin' to tie them on the backs of their horses and send them back to the Double X for a decent burial, Mr Bannister?' Jason asked.

Wendell shook his head. 'No, I'm going to bury them here somewhere and take the horses to the C L ranch. Slade's lost four men, two I shot dead earlier when they were trying to gun down a C L line-man. Slade will be wondering where they are. He'll guess they've been killed, but men like Slade don't plan for uncertainties.' Wendell smiled at Jason. 'He's due to start fretting about another two uncertainties.'

After the Millars had left them to go back to their shack, Wendell looked at Billy Jayhawk. 'I'd be obliged if you could go back on the ridge and see to that fella lying up there. I take it he's due for planting?' Billy grinned. Wendell nodded curtly. 'Nothing fine, Billy; drop him in some crack in the ground and cover him with rocks. That's more than Cassidy would have done for us if

181

he had come out on top. Mr Tilman, you can go and round up his horse.'

Mike wasn't hearing him. All smiles, he had seen Kath, hair flying wild, running towards him.

'OK, Mr Tilman,' Wendell said straight-faced. 'Go and put her mind at rest, show her you're still alive. Me and Mr Jayhawk will do the chores.'

★ ★ ★

When Wendell and the two young *compadres* set off to ride for the C L ranch, Jason Millar and five other sheepherders rode with them. One of the five was old Valdez, who admitted that while he wasn't much use with a rifle or a gun, he could still be of some help knowing the hidden trails through the mountains. Wendell hadn't turned him down. If young boys were willing to fight, who was he then to prevent a man old enough to be his grandpappy from playing his part in the coming struggle?

Another ten men in the settlement,

refusing to be intimidated by Slade, would mount a twenty-four hour guard along the ridge as a deterrent against any more attacks by the Double X crew. Wendell didn't think the rancher would pull off another 'stampede' ploy, but he could send men in on a burning-out raid.

Jason had been proved right, Wendell thought, as he sized up his small band. He gave a satisfied grunt. The sheepherder had said that most of the men in the settlement would stand tall when they were faced with the choice of fighting or eating crow. Only four familes had decided that sheep farming in the valley wasn't worth all the harassment and danger it brought and packed up what serviceable possessions they had left and set off to walk south back into California.

Wendell knew it was up to him now. He had to convince Al Brown that the only way he could hold on to his spread was to join forces with men to whom he wouldn't offer a drink of water

Kath, gripping her mother's hand, saw them leave. She had two men to worry about now and the tears bubbled in her eyes. Mrs Millar gave her daughter's hand a reassuring squeeze. Smiling wanly she said, 'They'll both be all right, Kath. Mr Bannister seems a capable man and Billy Jayhawk has been running rings round the Double X men for years.' Though in truth Mrs Millar felt like shedding a few tears of her own. As a born plainswoman she had seen menfolk ride off with guns, to settle some dispute or other, to return strapped across the backs of their horses ready for burial. Not wanting to depress Kath more than she already was, she held back her tears.

13

Al Brown's face grew longer with anger and disbelief as Jason told him of the destruction of the settlement by stampeding cattle. Wendell and the settlement party, along with Brown's straw boss, Boyce, were cramped in the main room in the ranch house, Wendell literally feeling the distrust and the animosity the two factions had for each other.

'So you can see our side in this matter, Mr Brown,' Jason continued. 'We're not about to put our lives on the line to make sure Slade is no longer a threat to us in the valley, only to find some other cattleman picks up where Slade leaves off and clears us off our land. I'd rather my people pull out of the valley and let you cattlemen continue to kill each other.'

'Mr Millar,' Brown said, 'I ain't

mealy-mouthed enough to say that cattlemen and sheepmen oughta be able to water their stock at the same waterin'-hole, but I don't crave your land, neither do my neighbours. We believe the territory is big enough for sheep and cattle. And, as God is my witness, I wouldn't stoop so low as to send cattle fire-ballin' into a settlement and risk the lives of women and children.'

'Good,' said a much relieved Wendell. There was still uneasiness in the air, which was understandable, he thought, knowing the tetchiness of the relation-ship between cattlemen and sheepmen, but the tension had gone. Neither side, he felt, was prepared to keep old feuds on the boil, in the grim situation facing them and fight their own separate battles.

'Now we're all on the same side,' he said, 'It's time we discussed tactics, try and catch Slade off guard while he's enjoying the thought he's cleared Jason's people out of the valley. And before he hears the bad news of his two hired guns being killed. Lovell, the other pistolero, thanks to young Mr Tilman there, is out of action, so we've only got the Double X crew to face. Some of them might not stay loyal to Slade when they see that things aren't going their boss's way.'

'Not all of Slade's crew are hard men, Mr Bannister,' Al Brown said. 'I reckon a few might quit his payroll if it came to an all-out shootin' war.'

'That's something I want to avoid,' replied Wendell. 'A face-to-face shoot-out outside Slade's front porch. I don't want either you or Mr Millar to lose any men. The two youngsters have showed us what our tactics should be by burning down one of Slade's barns right under his nose. We'll organize small hit-and-run raids. Strike Slade where he hit you, Mr Brown, the line cabins. Burn them down, take prisoner any of the crew there, and send the cows they were watching over scattering to the hills east of here. That's the way I see it, Mr Brown, but I'm willing to listen to anyone else's ideas.'

'It sounds good to me, Mr Bannister,' replied Brown. 'It oughta get that sonuvabitch Slade climbin' up the walls of his grand house madder than hell. For once in his life he ain't the one jerkin' the strings and makin' other people jump.'

Wendell glanced enquiringly at Jason Millar. Both men had to be with him, wholeheartedly. It was a wild-ass plan he had proposed and would need the co-operation of all in the room for it to have the chance of success.

Jason nodded his agreement. 'I read somewhere that attacking is the best form of defence,' he said. 'It kinda wrong-foots your enemy.' He looked at Mike. 'You were right, Mr Tilman. Weak as we felt we were, compared to Slade's crew, we oughta have got up from our asses and made a fight of it. Let's do it as you say, Mr Bannister.'

'Go and tell the cook to rustle up some chow for our pards, Boyce,' Al

Brown said. 'We're eatin' early. Then have the crew come up here, armed and ready to move out.' He wolf-grinned. 'I'm eager to see Slade's grand notion of bein' the cattle-king of the whole territory go up in flames. And I mean real ass-lickin' flames.'

* * *

By dusk, fed and saddled-up, and loaded for bear, the unlikely alliance of cattlemen and sheepmen was ready to settle their dispute with Slade once and for all. Impassive-faced, they knew the time for doubts and concerns was gone as they listened to Wendell's final orders. All determined that if they failed in their effort, the Double X crew would pay dearly for their victory.

'I think it's wise to split up your men, Mr Millar, with the ranch hands; those boys know the territory. Being I ought to earn the money Mr Brown pays me, I figure I should go for the furthest line cabin. And not wanting to get myself lost, Mr Jayhawk will ride with me. I'll also take Mr Tilman; those two young hell-raisers work well together.' Wendell grinned. 'They'll make sure an old man doesn't ride blindly into trouble again.' Serious-faced once more, Wendell continued issuing his orders. 'Don't set fire to the cabins until you see mine going up in flames,' he said. He paused for a few seconds but heard no questioning voice raised. 'One final point, shoot if you have to,' he said grimly. 'Your lives come first. It hasn't been officially declared, but it is war we're embarking on, gents. OK, that's all the talking done. Let's go and light some fires and see if it brings peace to the valley a great deal closer.'

★　★　★

Slade was enjoying his evening cigar sitting on his front porch. The good news he had been told by Simpson that the settlement had been flattened to the ground and the sheepherders demoralized and ready for quitting the valleys brought a nice inner glow of a job well done inside him. Though it was slightly tempered by the fact that Cassidy and Peckham hadn't brought in Billy Jayhawk and the Eastern dude kid.

'Those two hardcases will bring in the kids, Mr Slade,' Simpson had told him. 'But it could take some time. That 'breed's here there and everywhere.'

It was still light enough for Slade to see some way along the trail that led to the big house and at any moment he hoped to see his hired guns hauling in the two kids. Once he had seen them strung up he would take the war back again to the small spread men. This business, Slade thought, had gone on too long. He wanted his cattle grazing on their land before the winter snows swept along the valley.

14

Billy Jayhawk drew up his horse sharply and nodded skywards. 'It'll be as light as day down here soon, Mr Bannister,' he said. 'Men up on horses will be seen from miles away.'

Wendell swore softly. The boy was right. In a couple of minutes or so, the the moon would break through the clouds and on the open plain every tree, patch of brush, or rider, would be clearly seen. And that was bad business for men who wanted their presence to remain secret to the men they were going to jump until it was too late for their intended victim to do anything about it but submit without a fight. It was a pity, Wendell thought, they couldn't be all that far away from the line cabin he had planned to put to the torch.

The last of his small band of raiders,

working in groups of three, had left them to attack their target cabins and Wendell, not hearing any sounds of gunfire, took it that all the raids were being carried out successfully. And riding in moonlight bright enough to read a newspaper by wasn't the best way to ensure he and the two boys could carry out their tasks and return to the C L ranch unharmed. He sighed.

'OK, boys, dismount,' he said. 'Billy, find us some low ground to move along, fast and undetected. The fire-raisers back there will be waiting impatiently with lighted matches in their hands for us to set the ball rolling.'

Mike had had some experience of Billy Jayhawk's tracking skills in moving across hostile territory unseen, and he hoped his partner hadn't lost any of them. If they bumped into a bunch of Double X men they would have to do either of two things: have a stand-up gunfight, or ride like hell for safety, neither of which Mike knew he was much good at, even though now it wasn't so painful for him to sit up on a moving horse. Fortunately a cloud blew over, blanketing the moon and Billy judged it dark enough to get back on their mounts and to press on at some speed.

They heard and smelt the cattle first, then, circling the small band of longhorns, saw the dim yellow square of a lamp-lit cabin window.

'OK, *amigos*,' Wendell said. 'We go in on foot. You tend the horses, Mr Tilman, while me and Billy do what we came here to do.'

On coming up to the shack, Wendell told Billy to prepare a torch, light it throw it through the window. 'Then,' he said, 'you drop low and yell out, 'It's burning, Wendell, let's get the hell out of here'.' Wendell grinned. 'I'll be waiting by the door ready to cold-cock that fella inside when he comes bursting out to escape being roasted.'

It was a good, simple plan, Wendell thought, and would have worked if the Double X man hadn't decided to step outside to relieve himself. The sudden shaft of lamplight through the open door shone directly on to Billy Jayhawk down on his knees tugging up tufts of dry grass for his torch. The ranch hand cursed loudly and leapt back into the cabin, kicking the door shut with his boot. Wendell heard a locking bar being dropped in place, and did some cursing of his own. Wendell and Billy Jayhawk ate dirt.

The next sound they heard was the shattering of the window and the nonstop bark of a fourteen-load Winchester being emptied in their general direction. Then the cabin lamp was extinguished.

'Billy!' Wendell called out softly, 'we can either pull back before that damn moon breaks through allowing that fella inside to have two clear targets, or we can stay and burn down that shack as we intended.'

Billy looked skywards. 'We ain't got any length of time to discuss our options, Mr Bannister, so I say, bein' we're here, let's warm the Double X man's ass. And beside, those boys we dropped back along the trail will be waitin' for our signal, this cabin goin' up in flames, to start their own fires.'

'My way of thinking as well, Mr Jayhawk,' Wendell said. 'Now you get yourself at that door and get ready to put that man to sleep when he comes out. I'm going up on the roof to drop a few of these down the chimney. He'll think it's the fourth of July come early, right inside his cabin.'

Billy heard the clinking of shotgun shells in Wendell's hands.

'OK, Billy, let's do it,' Wendell said. And they both sped, crouched low in a weaving run, towards the cabin, eyes fixed on the broken window from where death could flame out at them.

The sudden burst of rifle fire almost caused Mike to drop the horse's reins, instinctively going down on to his knees as the shells whined through the dark away to his left. He had heard no cries of pain from either of his two partners so he guessed they had not been hit. Though, he thought soberly, a man killed instantly would have had no time to cry out. Mike wondered if he should leave the horses and go to see if he could be of any use to Mr Bannister and Billy Jayhawk, but he had the sense to realize wandering about in the dark would be of no help at all. He drew out his pistol and tightened his grip on the reins.

The noise Wendell made scrambling on to the low-pitched roof, with a help up from Billy Jayhawk, brought more wild rifle fire from the window. It wouldn't be wild, Billy thought grimly, once the moon came out and if Mr Bannister's scheme didn't work, forcing them to cut and run for it.

A panting, out-of-breath Wendell dropped lightly from the roof alongside Billy. 'Get ready, *amigo*,' he said. 'When the fireworks start popping that fella will come out fast. You'll only get one chance to bring him down.'

Murray, the Double X line man,

stood at one side of the window gazing at the roof, listening hard. If he could pick out exactly where the bastard on the roof was he would pump a full load of Winchester shells around his ass. Murray didn't know how many there were of the raiders but he was in no doubt why they were here. The sons-of-bitches were copying Slade's tactics, burning down the opposition's line cabins. He smiled coldly. He had plenty of shells and the cabin was stoutly built and he could hold off the C L crew until daylight. Then, if they showed as much as an inch of their dirty hides, he would put a hole through them.

Murray still gazed, puzzled-faced at the roof, wondering how the man up there was going to get at him. After the morning's storm the roof was too wet to burn, and if he tried to prise away any of the roof planks he would get the chance to blow his head off. Then the rattling of what sounded like stones dropping down the chimney of the old pot-bellied stove burning brightly in the centre of the cabin puzzled him still further.

Murray's 'what-the-hell?' look changed suddenly to one of fearful understanding as he realized just what he had thought to be stones, were. He had only time to kick the table on its side and fling himself down behind it when, with an ear-drumming bang, the stove blew apart. As though discharged from a field-piece, bits of burning logs, shards of red-hot metal, sprayed across the cabin, embedding into the walls and starting small, fast-burning fires. Some fell on Murray.

Cursing with pain, he got to his feet, shaking himself like a dog to get rid of the red-hot embers on his back. Gasping for breath in the throat-gagging thick soot and dust-cloud filling the room, he staggered to the door, gripping his pistol, blood mad with rage, and, as an ex-border hard man, determined to make a fight of it.

Lifting the bar Murray yanked open

the door and stepped outside shouting obscenities. Unable to see clearly, his vision blinded by smoke tears, he fired blindly right and left of him. Billy Jayhawk flinched as a shell thunked into the side of the cabin close to his head. With no chance of using his pistol as a club to knock out the Double X man, he triggered off two Colt rounds.

By the muzzle flash of his second shot, Billy saw the man fold up at the middle and sink to the ground. He stepped the few paces to the body, nudging it with the toe of his boot. He couldn't take a chance with a man crazy enough to come out fighting odds he must know he hadn't a chance to beat.

'Good work, Mr Jayhawk,' he heard Wendell say. 'Don't fret any, you had to do it. The sonuvabitch chose the hard way out. Now, let's get this cabin burning real good, we've been held up long enough.'

* * *

They were mounted up again, the shack behind them a raging wall of spark-crackling flames. Ahead of them, in the far distance, they saw the flickering red streaks, lighting up the low clouds, of the other line cabins being destroyed.

'A good night's work has been done tonight, *amigos*,' Wendell said. 'You boys ride back to the C L ranch. Slade will be in one helluva temper. They are bound to have seen the fires from the Double X, so tell Mr Brown to have his boys keep a sharp lookout till daybreak just in case Slade launches a full-scale raid against him.'

'Ain't you ridin' back with us, Mr Bannister?' Mike asked.

'No,' Wendell replied. 'The night's work isn't over for me yet.' He grinned at Mike. 'I have another plan, one I didn't tell you about at Brown's ranch house. I'm going to drive Slade down to his knees. Do what you and Billy had in mind, burn down his big house.'

'That's kinda stickin' your neck out a long ways, Mr Bannister,' Mike said.

'I'm a hired gun, Mr Tilman,' Wendell said. 'Paid to settle Mr Brown's trouble with Slade. I opine I have more than a fair chance to do that now.'

Billy Jayhawk didn't say anything. Attempting to burn down the Slade ranch house wasn't such a risky enterprise as Mike imagined. The Double X would be in an uproar, Slade yelling out orders, men riding out to see the extent of the damage to the line cabins, and a man as sneaky in moving around as Mr Bannister, if his luck held, could get in close enough to the house to set alight to it. Though Billy Jayhawk didn't reckon much on Mr Bannister's chances of making it back to the C L ranch safely. No man could bank on all the luck that would need. Unless he had help and the old pistolero was too proud to ask for it.

'OK, Mr Tilman,' he said. 'Let's move out; Mr Bannister needs all the night hours he can get. We'll see you at the C L ranch, Mr Bannister.' He pulled his horse's head around calling out as he did so, 'The best of luck, pard!'

Mike followed him, albeit reluctantly. Once out of earshot of Wendell, he scowled fiercely at Billy Jayhawk. 'To hell with what he said, we shoulduv gone with him. We're supposed to be what you Westerners call pards, ain't we?'

Billy Jawhawk grinned. 'We are goin' with the old man, pard,' he said. 'Though he don't know it yet. If we cut round to the left of that stand of timber we'll beat our pard to Slade's ranch house, in time to see he don't land himself into trouble he can't pull out of. But remember my earlier warnin': if I go to ground, you do likewise. There's bound to be Double X men ridin' this way soon.'

15

Wendell looked down from the rim of a small ridge at all the activity going on at the ranch house. The burning line cabins, seen as dim red glow from where he was, had sure stirred up one hell of a hornet's nest, he thought. Lamplights were showing through all the ground-floor windows of the house and he could see men coming to get their orders from a big bulky man standing on the front porch, then mounting their horses to ride off somewhere. Wendell opined the big man was Slade and, the way he was heavy-footing up and down the porch his cabins going up in flames had given him a lot to chew over, all of it unpleasant to his taste.

★ ★ ★

Slade found it hard to think coherently. A nervous tic throbbed on the right side of a red-mottled angry face. The whole damn valley had been within his grasp, he thought bitterly. He was the man who gave out the 'do this or else' ultimatum, and now, within a few days, he was being forced into a corner, fighting in a conflict he no longer controlled.

Slade knew, as if he had been told, that Cassidy and Peckham were as dead as Curly and Mel. And it was almost a certainty the line men whose cabins he had been dragged out of bed and told were burning, were also dead. He was losing men he couldn't afford to lose if he wanted to be the only rancher in the valley.

Slade gave a derisive sob of a laugh. Simpson had told him the stampede had broken the sheepherders yet he could feel it in his guts the broken-backed sons-of-bitches were out there helping Al Brown to burn down his cabins. He put his sudden change of fortune down to Wendell Bannister. The killing of his men and the burning-out raids had his mark on them. By what he had heard of him, when he took part in a range war the bodies of the men he was hired to fight would soon be piled high. Slade's face twisted into an angry snarl. But the fancy-shooting Bannister hadn't finished him yet. As soon as it was light he would round-up as many of his crew as he could spare, and that included the hired gun, Lovell, nursing his swollen balls in the bunkhouse, and wipe Al Brown, his ranch, his whole damn crew off the face of the territory. Then he would hit the sheepherders so hard those that could wouldn't stop running until they had crossed the California line. Those confident thoughts lowered Slade's blood pressure somewhat.

★   ★   ★

The rear of the ranch house was in darkness and all quiet and Wendell had

206

no difficulty in getting in close to it without shouts of alarm being raised, then gunfire coming his way. The bunkhouse, close by the house, was lit up and its door was wide open. By what was going on at the front of the house, Wendell didn't think any of the crew would be inside. Slade, he reckoned, would even have the ranch cook armed and mounted up ready for action. He stood and listened but hearing no talk or sounds of movement inside the hut, he made the twenty or so yard dash to the ranch house and, pushing open a door, slipped inside.

Wendell rested with his back against a wall of what he could see was the kitchen to allow his heartbeat to return to normal. Here in the kitchen he could see there was plenty of material, cooking oil, boxes, paper, to start a blaze that would take hold of the main structure of the building, though he had to move fast before the good stroke of luck he was being favoured with ran out. He laid his shotgun on a table and, opening a tin of oil, began to pour it across the floor and chairs.

'Do you think Mr Bannister made it, Billy?' Mike said. 'I can't see him.'

The pair of them were bellied down in the same spot they had been lying in the night they had burned down the barn.

'Of course we can't see him,' Billy replied sarcastically. 'Mr Bannister's makin' sure he ain't seen. If we see him so could some of the Double X men and we would have been hearin' gunfire as we came in.' He grinned at Mike. 'But my ma's blood tells me he's here. He'll be sneakin' about at the rear of the ranch house; it's dark there. We don't want to be movin' around, so we'll lie doggo ready to back him up if things go wrong for him.'

Wendell took a satisfied look at his handiwork. The oil had been well splashed around the room and once he put a match to the pile of papers underneath the table he would have to make a quick getaway if he didn't want to be roasted alive by the inferno he was about to start. Then things went all wrong for Wendell in the shape of an evil-grinning Lovell standing in the doorway with his pistol trained on him. He cursed and made a grab for his shotgun, but Lovell put a bullet in his arm smashing his shoulder. Face white with pain, he clutched at his wounded arm glaring back at Lovell.

Lovell had been making his slow painful way to the ranch house to tell Slade he wanted to ride with the rest of the boys.

Shooting dead some sheepherder or cow hand would take his mind off the pain he was suffering. Lovell didn't believe in God, or miracles but on seeing Bannister skulking across to the ranch house he thought he ought to take up religion. Cass and Peckham were about to meet up with the no-good sonuvabitch he didn't doubt; Bannister had jumped them somehow and shot them down.

'Take that pistol out nice and slow,

Bannister,' Lovell said. 'For I have a great urge to put you down for keeps as I reckon you've done for Cass and Peckham, but the man who's payin' me will take great pleasure in stringin' you up.'

Slade and his straw boss, with guns drawn, burst into the kitchen on hearing the shot, Slade wondering frantically what other trouble could have landed on him.

'This is Wendell Bannister, Mr Slade,' Lovell said. 'The man who I reckon stirred up all this trouble for you.'

Slade smiled, a real, relieved smile. Without the killer instincts of the man now his prisoner, the opposition against him would fold up. Lovell deserved a bonus.

Mike jerked his head round in alarm to look at Billy, the shot spelt big trouble for Mr Bannister. He was just in time to see his partner heading fast towards the rear of the house. He got to his feet and took off after him.

'I've drawn his claws, Mr Slade,' Lovell said. 'His pistol's lyin' there at his feet and the fancy scatter-gun he favours is on the table.' He grinned. 'And he knows that if he so much as gives me an unkind look I'll put a shell right between his eyes.'

Slade and Simpson holstered their pistols, Slade fish-eying Wendell. 'Mr Bannister,' he said, 'you've caused me a great deal of trouble, but you haven't stopped what Al Brown paid you for, only delayed it a spell. This valley is still going to be mine! Bring the sonuvabitch out front, Lovell, there's a fine tree standing there, planted by my pa, with a branch strong enough to hang a dirty no-good shootist!'

Wendell shivered with fear. He had expected some day, when his gun arm slowed down, that some up-and-coming pistolero would beat him to the draw. But to be strung up like a goddamned cattle thief scared the hell out of him. Though he wasn't about to show his fears to his captors.

'You're finished, Slade!' he said, sounding more bold than he was feeling. 'It's only because you haven't got the savvy to realize it yet. The C L crew have joined up with the sheepherders and are fighting back, and tasting the sweetness of victory. There's no stopping them now; they'll come here and hit you hard. Then you could find that some of your boys haven't got the stomach for a fight they know they're losing.'

Slade gave Wendell a mad-eyed glare. 'Get the rope, Simpson,' he snarled. 'And let's get this business over with. We've a heavy day comin' up!'

Billy paused before he opened the ranch-house door. Face all Paiute he looked at Mike. 'We're steppin' into a hell of a gunfight once we walk through this door, pard,' he said. 'If you want to back out, I won't hold it agin you. Bein' an Easterner, you won't be used to suchlike shootin' parties.'

Mike matched Billy's stone-carved face with a stubborn hardness of his own. 'Have no doubts on my score, pard.' Mike tapped his shotgun. 'I'll kill if I have to. And if Mr Bannister's lyin' dead in there I'll make sure we'll finish off what he came here to do, burn this place down.'

Billy grinned. 'I never doubted your intentions, pard.' Face Indianed up again, he said, 'Let's pay our respects to Mr 'High and Mighty' Slade,' and kicked open the door and sprang inside the room.

Billy read the scene inside the room in an instant. The big man whirling round to face him was the only one of the three Double X men with a gun in his hand. 'Cover those two assholes, Mike!' he yelled, above the roar of his pistol, sending three shells into the surprised-faced Lovell.

Lovell fell heavily across the table, slipping off it, dead, to land on the floor. Billy stepped over the body, further into the room, giving him a clear shooting angle at Slade and Simpson. Without taking his eyes off them, he said, 'Are you OK, Mr Bannister?'

'Yeah, I'm OK, Mr Jayhawk,' Wendell groaned. He managed a ghost of a smile. 'I'm feeling a damn sight better than Lovell lying there with his chest stove in.'

Slade's dreams of a cattle empire stretching the whole length of the valley were shattered again. Face contorted in wild rage, he clawed for his pistol.

Mike, hands sticky on the stock of the shotgun, whether from fear or excitement he was in no state to judge, glimpsed Slade's desperate move and pulled back both triggers of the gun. The lead hail cut the front of Slade's fancy frilled shirt into bloody ribbons. The force of the close-range shot flung the rancher back hard against the wall, there to slide down slowly, leaving a bloody smear on the wall, landing on the floor in a sitting position, chin resting on his chest.

A strained-faced Simpson had heard the two kids were wild and deadly, and he had just witnessed how deadly they were. Slowly he raised his hands. 'You'll get no grief from me, boys,' he croaked.

'Reload that cannon of yours, Mr Tilman,' Wendell said, his gun back in his hand again. 'And blast away at anyone coming through that door, OK?'

'OK, Mr Bannister,' replied Mike, thumbing reloads into the shotgun chambers, and trying not to look at the man he had almost cut in two.

'And you, Mr Jayhawk,' Wendell said. 'I'd be obliged if you'd do likewise with the back door.'

Wendell turned and faced Simpson. 'The man who paid your wages is dead, Simpson,' he said. 'Are you as ambitious as he was? Or do we have peace in the valley? I reckon Slade's caused enough bloodshed, but if you're a prodding man like your boss was then I'll oblige you with a war. I'll start by burning down this fine house which is what I came here to do. It only needs a lighted match dropped on this floor and believe me there'll be one hell of a conflagration.' Wendell close-eyed him. 'What's it going to be, Mr Simpson?'

Simpson lowered his hands. He pointed to the dead Lovell. 'He was the last of the men paid to fight, me and the rest of the crew only did so out of loyalty to Slade. Now he's dead there ain't any reason left for us to put our necks on the line.' He smiled. 'I ain't got any burnin' ambition to be cattle baron, Mr Bannister. I've got my bellyful bein' straw boss of this outfit, hopin' I'll still be one when whoever of Slade's kin takes over the ranch. The killing's over.'

Relief flooded over Wendell. 'OK, *amigos*, lower your guns. We'll take Mr Simpson's word, the trouble's over. We'll let him clean up the mess here and let's get back to the C L.' Wendell forced another smile on his pain-drawn face. 'Your future pa-in-law, Mike, will be worrying if you're OK or not. And you, Mr Jayhawk, could favour me again by making sure I stay in the saddle on the ride back. One time a lump of lead in my hide wouldn't have troubled me, but now it's hurting like hell. I must be getting old.'

★ ★ ★

It was a much more cheerful band of sheepherders who rode back to the settlement. They all knew the hard, sweat-raising work they would have to put in to rebuild their homes but the nervous, over-the-shoulder looks for signs of raiding cattlemen were gone. Al Brown was no Slade.

Mike had his own private, pleasant thoughts occupying his mind. He had decided to stay here in the valley and to hell with the long trip back to New York. If he had met up with all the trouble he had just come through only a hundred or so miles from 'Frisco what could be waiting for him further East, and with no friends to back him up? He would never make it to New York. Besides his future wife was here, so was his *amigo*, Billy Jayhawk, who had given up stealing cattle and would now be on the C L payroll. And Mr Bannister was also staying with Mr Brown until his wound healed and he felt the need to move on. Mike grinned to himself. And at last he had got his saddle-ass.

'Let's give the boys on the ridge the good news,' Jason said, as the rise came into view. He raised his hat and started cheering, and the rest of the men followed suit. Mike cheered, feeling as though he had been part of the sheepherder fraternity for years.

Jason grinned at Mike. 'Ma's lost one worry, son,' he said. 'But she's about to get another frettin' session, rustlin' up a weddin' dress for Kath.'

Mike beamed. 'Does that mean you're invitin' me to stay at the settlement, Pa?'

'You'd better had, son,' Jason said. 'Or Ma and Kath will never speak to me again.'

We do hope that you have enjoyed reading this large print book.

Did you know that all of our titles are available for purchase?

We publish a wide range of high quality large print books including:
Romances, Mysteries, Classics
General Fiction
Non Fiction and Westerns

Special interest titles available in large print are:
The Little Oxford Dictionary
Music Book, Song Book
Hymn Book, Service Book

Also available from us courtesy of Oxford University Press:
Young Readers' Dictionary
(large print edition)
Young Readers' Thesaurus
(large print edition)

For further information or a free brochure, please contact us at:
Ulverscroft Large Print Books Ltd.,
The Green, Bradgate Road, Anstey,
Leicester, LE7 7FU, England.
Tel: (00 44) **0116 236 4325**
Fax: (00 44) **0116 234 0205**

A TOWN CALLED TROUBLESOME

John Dyson

Matt Matthews had carved his ranch out of the wild Wyoming frontier. But he had his troubles. The big blow of '86 was catastrophic, with dead beeves littering the plains, and the oncoming winter presaged worse. On top of this, a gang of desperadoes had moved into the Snake River valley, killing, raping and rustling. All Matt can do is to take on the killers single-handed. But will he escape the hail of lead?

CABEL

Paul K. McAfee

Josh Cabel returned home from the Civil War to find his family all murdered by rioting members of Quantrill's band. The hunt for the killers led Josh to Colorado City where, after months of searching, he finally settled down to work on a ranch nearby. He saved the life of an Indian, who led him to a cache of weapons waiting for Sitting Bull's attack on the Whites. His involvement threw Cabel into grave danger. When the final confrontation came, who had the fastest — and deadlier — draw?

RIVERBOAT

Alan C. Porter

When Rufus Blake died he was found to be carrying a gold bar from a Confederate gold shipment that had disappeared twenty years before. This inspires Wes Hardiman and Ben Travis to swap horse and trail for a riverboat, the *River Queen*, on the Mississippi, in an effort to find the missing gold. Cord Duval is set on destroying the *River Queen* and he has the power and the gunmen to do it. Guns blaze as Hardiman and Travis attempt to unravel the mystery and stay alive.

McKINNEY'S LAW

Mike Stotter

McKinney didn't count on coming across a dead body in the middle of Texas. He was about to become involved in an ever-deepening mystery. The renegade Comanche warrior, Black Eagle, was on the loose, creating havoc; he didn't appear in McKinney's plans at all, not until the Comanche forced himself into his life. The US Army gave McKinney some relief to his problems, but it also added to them, and with two old friends McKinney set about bringing justice through his own law.

BLACK RIVER

Adam Wright

John Dyer has come to the insignificant little town of Black River to destroy the last living reminder of his dark past. He has come to kill. Jack Hart is determined to stop him. Only he knows the terrible truth that has driven Dyer here, and he knows that only he can beat Dyer in a gunfight. Ex-lawman Brad Harris is after Dyer too — to avenge his family. The stage is set for madness, death and vengeance.